KU-065-219

No.1 CREATOR OF HOSPITAL NOVELS

IN AN EDINBURGH DRAWING ROOM

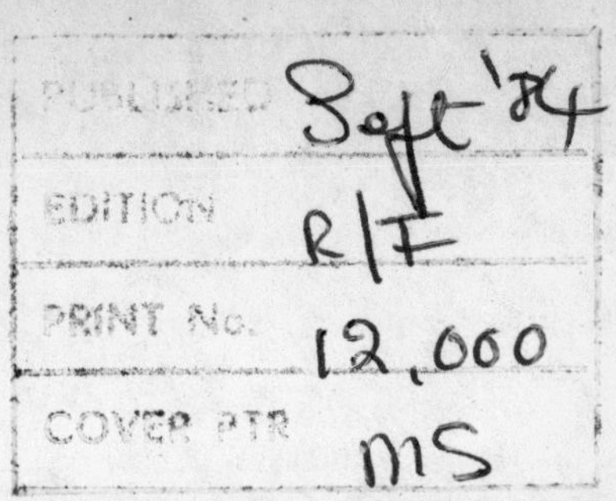

IN AN EDINBURGH DRAWING ROOM

Britain, midwinter 1980-81. Before the New Year arrives, the lives of four young people will be transformed by the violence that precipitates three into the life and care of the fourth, Mary Hogg, senior staff nurse in an Intensive Therapy Unit of a small northern English hospital.

With this novel Lucilla Andrews completes the story begun in *One Night in London* and continued in *A Weekend in the Garden*, where George MacDonald's love for Catherine Jason, née Carter, led to a long and happy marriage, built on the ashes of their shattered pasts as successfully as the great new St Martha's has risen from the bomb-damaged rubble of the old – and young Mary Hogg over her tragically deprived childhood.

In An Edinburgh Drawing Room is a story of courage and love, and of hope for the future that, as ever, lies in the hands of the young.

Also by Lucilla Andrews

A WEEKEND IN THE GARDEN
THE PRINT PETTICOAT

and published by Corgi Books

In an Edinburgh Drawing Room

Lucilla Andrews

IN AN EDINBURGH DRAWING ROOM

A CORGI BOOK 0 552 12439 7

Originally published in Great Britain by William Heinemann Ltd.

PRINTING HISTORY
William Heinemann edition published 1983
Corgi edition published 1984

This book is set in

Corgi Books are published by
Transworld Publishers Ltd.,
Century House, 61-63 Uxbridge Road,
Ealing, London W5 5SA

Made and printed in Great Britain by
Hunt Barnard Printing Ltd., Aylesbury, Bucks.

1

They should slap on a government health warning, thought Jason, dropping into his reserved backward-facing seat that afternoon. They should slap it up over the main entrance to Accidents and Emergencies: 'DANGER: HM Govt. Health Depts. WARNING: ADMISSION TO HOSPITAL ON SUNDAY EVENINGS MAY SERIOUSLY DAMAGE YOUR HEALTH.' And as the train had already begun to pull out of King's Cross, he rested his black head against the high, padded back of his seat, half-closed his bloodshot, dark blue eyes and thought with weary, ambivalent gratitude of 'Mrs Jim'. She was a nice old soul and she'd gone to a lot of trouble, but he wished to God she hadn't.

'Mrs Jim', a former senior ward sister in Martha's, had returned to working part time as a staff nurse in A. and E. after she had raised a family and her husband had retired. 'A man likes his kitchen to himself, Mr MacDonald, and we all know what gin costs now. But what's this I hear about your not having booked your seat up on the 30th? Dear boy, do you really want to stand to Edinburgh after working over Christmas? It's probably too late but I'm off early this afternoon. Let me see what I can fix . . . I insist!' On the following day she had presented him with a seat reservation ticket. 'Had to be a first smoker on the 15.45 extra. Only first smokers left on that and everything on all the later trains booked solid. I thought I'd better grab it. I *know* you're on that weekend – see what we can fix. Put it away in your wallet . . .' – from her attitude he was seven, not twenty-seven, an FRCS of a few months' standing and temporarily acting Senior Accident Officer – '. . . and when you get home do give my regards to your parents. Of course they won't remember me! I was only a third year when your mother came back to staff in the general theatre in' 48 when – er – when your father was our newest general surgical pundit. This was before they married – back in the dark ages to you young things. Your father gave my set our general surgical lectures and at my present great age I don't mind admitting that Mack – as all Martha's called him behind his back – was our pin-up! How we wasted energy making up clean caps for his lectures and flapping our eyelashes at him! Loaded with SA that man – or shouldn't I tell his son so? Anyway. I have – and you can tell them I was Barrard. Monica Barrard. No use giving them my married name. Won't mean a thing and best forgotten as I committed the most heinous crime any Martha of my era could short of deliberately murdering a patient. Married one. The dregs, Mr MacDonald, the dregs!'

Jason smiled faintly at the speeding suburbs. The old girl had hit A. and E. like a Force 9. She knew her job, was reliable as hell, and having known all the Martha's qualified consultants as students or housemen, and been a ward sister when the present District Nursing Officer was taking O Levels and the Senior Nursing Officer in primary school, 'Mrs Jim' had no hesitation in making the kind of demands that from others would have caused vast umbrage, strikes, or both, and not just getting away with it, but getting her way. As today. A Monday.

In St Martha's Hospital, London, residents on weekend duty were on call from 9 a.m. Friday to 5 p.m. Monday. The new Accident Consultant wasn't a Martha's man, but just before lunch today he had swept into the SAO's office as if leading the Welsh pack against the English at Cardiff Arms. 'Just heard of your small problem, boyo. *No* problem. I'll take over from you at three. We all know what Hogmanay means to you Scots – the least one ethnic minority can do for another, Jason,' he added jovially. He prided himself on his common touch and the elderly staff nurse had just informed him – in strict confidence – that this young giant was his father's son. It hurt no man to do a good turn to those that had held high places and retained sufficient status to drop the right words in the right ears. 'Scrub last evening out of your mind. You did your best. No man can do more – not that there's one damn thing anyone can for those that shove their brains out of the back of their skulls. Get up home, enjoy yourself and have a few drams for me!'

Jason's well-chiselled, good-humoured lips tightened. Scrub the thought the young doctor's best wasn't bloody good enough. Hand him a bouquet. Come in handy as an extra wreath.

He closed his eyes but couldn't close out thought. Just two punk kids flogging the guts out of the machines they'd been given for Christmas – and he could still see what was left of their heads, and their parents' faces. He couldn't remember what he'd said to those parents, but he remembered being so tired that he had had to dredge up every word and from their expressions every one had been an obscenity. Right!

Saturday nights in A. and E. were usually rough; this last, coming between the two holidays, hit a new low. It had been 11 p.m. before they had cleared the consequences of the goalless draw of the replay on the ground nearest Martha's. Martha's score: 52 admitted injured; 43 discharged home after treatment in A. and E.; 5 transferred to Orthopaedic Unit; 4 transferred to Intensive Therapy Unit. And all evening and night; roads, muggings, fights, drunks, drugs. Clean up that bunch and the whole A. and E. staff would be in the dole queue.

Normal winter Sundays were fairly quiet; yesterday had been abnormal. But summer and winter, Monday was the heaviest working day of the A. and E. week. He had just got to lunch today when he was called back; he hadn't had time to return to finish the meal and had only caught the train by running from his taxi to a ticket office and then to the platform. When he leapt on he had been vaguely aware his seat was the only empty one around, but he hadn't bothered to notice the other passengers or the first swirls of cigarette smoke down this end, or remove his leather driving coat. He didn't smoke, but he was too tired to care if he reached Edinburgh with kippered lungs, or if his coat had him sweating by Peterborough.

All he wanted was sleep, but his overactive mind refused to switch off and insisted on rerunning Gill's telephone call from Edinburgh last night: 'I've swung it! Isn't it super! Aren't I clever! Aren't you impressed?' Impressed?

Christ. He'd just left those parents. God alone knew what he'd said to her. All he could remember about that part now was that his instinctive reaction to her news had been the strong urge to puke at himself. When she had rung off, he had been tempted for a few seconds to ring home with some excuse about having to stay on. That he had known his parents would accept it without offence or recrimination had deepened his sense of guilt and self-disgust. Then his bleeper had sounded off and he'd had to get back to the shop.

He blinked open his eyes and unwittingly glared blearily into the face the girl in the opposite single seat raised from her paperback. She met his glare coldly. 'This is the smoker's end,' she said, looking pointedly from her lighted cigarette to the blank pane of their wide, shared window.

He was too tired to register more than her English accent and darkish gold hair, and that she had the most glorious brown eyes he had ever seen in a woman. 'Not that. Hangover,' he muttered, closing his eyes to back up his story, and then falling asleep as if poleaxed. He slept so deeply that he never later recalled being superficially woken to show his ticket, or anything more until he woke suddenly in the violently swaying blackness and heard the shouts ands cries in the few seconds before he lost consciousness.

Francesca Turner was glad the large macho opposite had flaked out and that her father's secretary had booked her a single. She was in no mood to spend the next five or so hours blocking attempts to chat her up. Her seat was the last in the row of singles running up the right side of the long, warm carriage that was the second behind the engine. A narrow aisle divided singles from doubles and on both sides the seats were paired to face each other over fixed, waist-high table tops. At both ends of the carriage were luggage shelves and beyond them the self-operating electronic glass doors leading to the lavatories and the rest of the train. And as this was built for high speeds, the doors for passengers boarding and leaving the train lay on either side of the short transverse corridors off which lay the lavatories. Already, in most of the second class accommodation, these corridors were filled with passengers standing, sitting on their luggage, or on the floor.

The last doubles in the left row of the second carriage were shared by an elderly couple in the window seats and two schoolboys. The boys were patently brothers travelling independently, and from their heated whispered exchange on boarding, regarded the London–Edinburgh run as an extension of the school bus. '. . . you jolly well know it's my turn to face, Nige! And I'm not swopping first stop! I'll be sick as sick by York and you'll be snoring – you always snore and –'

'Not a 125, wet! Extra. First stop's Peterborough –'

'I know! I just forgot. Anyway it's *my turn* and –'

'Stuff it, Simon! Everyone's looking!' The older boy, who looked about fourteen, had flung himself into the seat beside the elderly man and mouthed an obscenity at his triumphant younger brother. Francesca Turner had controlled her amusement, opened her paperback, and hoped the old bat this side had never learnt to lip-read as she was already oozing enough disapproval to blow a blood-vessel.

Francesca Turner was twenty-two and had acquired a detached attitude to life that regularly caused her nursing authorities in the Murrayfield General Hospital, Edinburgh, to observe to each other that the girl might almost be a Scot. 'Such a canny cool head . . .' She lowered her book for a closer look at the macho. Quite tasty – if large dark lovely alcoholics were to your taste. No; that 'alcoholic' was a bit off. He wasn't a hooked Lunchtime O'Booze. No bags under the eyes, sagging jowls, or beer bulge; and as he looked in his late twenties or early thirties, by now habitual boozing would show. Probably just had to get tanked-up to face going home for Hogmanay. He'd the height, colouring and facial bone-structure of a highlander, but whether highland or lowland, he was bound to be going home. Three years in Edinburgh had taught her that the Scots regarded New Year's Eve as the English did Christmas Day; whether families loved or loathed each other, any member that avoided without accepted alibi the traditional family reunion bore the Mark of Cain not only in the coming year but in undimmed family memory. 'Oh yes, that was the year John/Angus, Mary/Margaret chose not to join the family circle . . . one knows the young must lead their own lives, but really . . .'

Thank God for the Scottish Hogmanay and that her father and latest stepmother were English. There'd been only a token scene about her returning today. 'We can't blame young Francesca, my sweet. No place like Scotland for seeing in the New Year – no wonder they need two bank holidays to sweat off the whisky!'

Francesca's mother had been the first of her father's four wives and had borne his only child in whom, Mr Turner told himself on the rare occasions when he recalled the child's existence, he would have taken interest had it been a son. But no one, he reassured himself with infinitely greater truth, could accuse him of not being a good paternal provider. His first, and only dead, former wife had been killed in a skiing accident when their daughter was two. Her death had made little impact on Francesca's life as by then her youngish nanny, Susan, had become her surrogate mother. Once Francesca was old enough for boarding school Susan had remained as housekeeper of the large country house in rural Kent that had been Francesca's home throughout her childhood and was the one of her father's three houses that he invariably used for Christmas but otherwise seldom visited. Ten years ago Susan had left to marry the local sub-postmaster-cum-general stores owner, but she had continued to be the one person in the world to whom Francesca regularly wrote and visited of her own accord. Yesterday she'd gone to tea with Susan.

'How about the new one, love?'

'My God, Susan, he's done it again. Lovely, loaded, her kids dumped on her ex and she's into her third.'

'I'll say this for your dad. He knows the value of money in and out of his business. Tell me about this flat he's bought you. Real nice, is it?'

'A snip. I don't really need my scooter now. Just a short walk up the hill to the hospital.'

'That's nice. And nice you've these two girls sharing. Been on your own too much, if you ask me. Nice pair, are they?'

'Nice enough. They needed digs and I had the room, so – well – in they came.'

'That's nice.' Susan concentrated on refilling their cups. 'They know what your dad's worth?'

'I'm not that daft.'

'You never were, love. That's your trouble. How about – er – boyfriends?'

'Do you mind! Only guys I seem to meet are medics, male nurses or oilmen. Yuck the lot! But some of the medic girls are quite decent.'

Susan glanced up. 'You thinking to turn doctor once you finish your nursing?'

Francesca nodded. 'Just for you.'

'You know me, love! And – er – how about the bad dreams?'

'Don't get them in Edinburgh.'

Susan looked at the small, slight girl's pale dark-eyed face that could look plain or beautiful. She saw the shadows under the eyes and sighed inwardly. 'Hate to see you go, love, but the sooner you get back up to your Scotch pals the better. Drop us a card to say you've arrived safe.'

'You know I will.'

From the opposite corner seat and the cover of an open, worn copy of *Barchester Towers*, Mr Halstead studied the brown-eyed blonde in a shapeless scarlet sweater and stained grey whipcords, with the discretion acquired from years of managing banks and over three decades of a marriage barren in every sense. Mr Halstead was a tall, heavy man with shrewd grey eyes tucked well back beneath thick grey brows, and neatly dressed crinkling grey hair. He had noticed the girl when he followed his wife into the carriage and had immediately been conscious of a sensation so long forgotten that he had mentally filed it to await investigation at the appropriate time. That time had to wait until he had attended to his wife's comfort, an exercise he had learnt to pursue without seeing her puckered, petulant face. He had long ceased to care for his wife but he cared for her comfort as she was his responsibility.

'All well, m'dear?' he had queried.

She had answered by directing an affronted glance at the stage-whispering boys. Mr Halstead had known she regarded their presence as a personal insult from which he should have spared her, but that knowledge no longer troubled him. He had learnt to accept that his wife required real or imaginary insults as others needed nicotine, or alcohol. In point of fact, he now reflected, after the initial fraternal spat the youngsters were proving remarkably unobjectionable. The little chap had become engrossed in his comics and his elder brother was beginning to nod off.

Would it have been different had they had children? He doubted it. As he had often observed to himself when watching clients over his office desk, children appeared to be expensive items that only cemented those marriages in no need of repair. He'd never known why they had been childless. During the appropriate time, his suggestions that they seek medical advice had so offended his wife that he had seen no alternative to dropping the subject and as time went by he had been relieved to recognise that his wife regretted their situation no more than himself. Certainly, children would have interfered with her coffee mornings, bridge club, and the impeccable order in which she had maintained their various homes during his professional life and the large bungalow at Wexhill-on-Sea that had been their home since he retired seven years ago. Providentially, the bungalow had a good garden and Wexhill an excellent golf course. 'I can't think what you'll do without the bank, Joe,' she used to say. 'Nothing to look forward to but boredom and cancer.' His dry retort, 'If I have the latter I doubt I'll suffer the former,' had been a mistake. She had never understood and always resented his sense of humour as it made her feel uncomfortable. 'If it's a joke, why aren't you laughing, Joe?' In the early years of their marriage he had tried gentle teasing – 'Joke coming, Peggy – wait for it . . .'– until her tightening mouth had taught him to keep his humour, as his thoughts, to himself.

Once, long ago – he glanced again at the lowered darkish gold head – long ago. He returned his gaze to his open book but didn't see Trollope's words that he knew almost by heart and were his preferred personal anodyne. He saw so vividly in memory a golden-haired dark-eyed girl in WREN's uniform that had he then glanced at his reflection in a mirror he would have been shocked that it was not that of a fresh-faced, fair-haired young man in a khaki battledress with two pips up. 'One day, Joe, we'll be away up to my folks in Gairlie. You've not seen Ben Gairlie? Man, you've not lived! You'll love the Ben . . .' No time for that. So much now. None, then. Jean, he thought, Jean Gordon. He had only known her for nine weeks but as those weeks had been the last of her short life he had remembered them for years after her death in one of the air-raids on Portsmouth. Throughout those years the sight of any small, slim, young dark-eyed blonde had made him wince. When he had married in 1949, his bride had been a tall, plump, strikingly attractive brunette.

Mrs Halstead exchanged *The Tatler* for *Vogue*, and, averting her eyes from the boys, cast an outraged glance at the sleeping young man. It was as obvious to her that he was drunk as that it was only a matter of time before he started shouting, singing, and being sick and the boys started making nuisances of themselves. Having the over-anxious temperament of the true egotist, Mrs Halstead invariably placed the worst construction on any situation and anticipated accordingly; in consequence, she was regarded by her bridge friends as a woman of rare perception as her views so frequently accorded with those of the world in general.

One just didn't expect this sort in the firsts. One usually had rather a nice sort even though so many on this run seemed to be Americans. Of course it was common knowledge that oilmen earned fortunes and one had to admit they seemed to know how to behave. Take those four just ahead talking so quietly one could only catch the odd word from the deep, drawling voices that were amusingly reminiscent of *Dallas* on TV. One did enjoy *Dallas*! But that wretched drunk wasn't in oil. Far too pale and from the look of his hands didn't know the meaning of a job of work. One couldn't imagine how he – or that scruffy girl who must have bought her clothes in a jumble sale – could afford to travel first. Just more examples of how the young always seemed to have enough money to do whatever they wanted these days despite all this talk of youth unemployment. If they were unemployed, one knew why. They didn't want to work and why should they whilst the government kept handing them out the taxpayers' money? All they wanted were rights without responsibilities, decided Mrs Halstead, who had moved from her father's to her husband's household and had never for one day in her life financially supported herself.

Her thoughts were agreeably interrupted by the woman rising from the seat immediately ahead of the drunk's and previously hidden by the seats' high backs. She was a tallish, slender woman with neat, greying brown hair and an authoritative air. She seemed to hesitate by the drunk before walking on out of the carriage.

Mrs Halstead's puffy-lidded hazel eyes brightened with interest and she leant her ample bosom on the table to whisper 'Joe. Joe!'

Mr Halstead turned reluctantly from the approaching outline of Peterborough cathedral that was dark grey against the paler grey sky. 'Eh? Yes, m' dear?'

'I've just recognised the woman sitting in front of . . .' She gestured distastefully. 'She's just gone out. One wasn't surprised she looked taken aback by . . .' (another gesture). 'She's Dame Ruth Dean. Look when she comes back. She's in blue tweeds.'

The thick grey brows met. 'How do you know?'

'Why do you never remember anything I tell you? Surely you remember when we were up with Margaret last summer she took me as her guest to that meeting at the Murrayfield General – the day you had a golf tournament – and this Dame Ruth Dean was the speaker. I know I told you.'

'No doubt, m'dear. Why's she a DBE?'

'She's a terribly VIP nurse – used to be Matron of St Martha's – *the* St Martha's – only they're not called Matrons now. Margaret said she sits on government committees and working parties and that sort of thing. She wore a sort of blue floral tent last summer – can't imagine why as she's one of the lucky ones and hasn't lost her figure.'

Purely for the sake of domestic peace, on the return of the woman in a blue tweed jacket and skirt, Mr Halstead scrutinised her discreetly and formed the opinion that he would have no hesitation in allowing her to overdraw within reasonably generous limits, in the highly unlikely event of the owner of that calm, strong face seeking such an indulgence. But – and he twisted his head for closer inspection – even in a speeding train she knew how to move and had quite remarkable legs for a woman of her, or come to that, any age. He turned quickly back to his wife in conditioned, if totally unsuspected guilt and offered to get her a cup of tea from the buffet car. 'And a couple of biscuits?'

'Trust you to forget my new diet! Anyhow, I'm not thirsty. I'll wait till York.' She didn't enquire if he wanted any refreshment, but neither noticed. Joe, she repeatedly assured her widowed sister-in-law Margaret Goodwin with whom they were spending the next week, enjoyed fending for himself. And Margaret Goodwin, having throughout her marriage regarded her late husband's stomach as her personal property and responsibility, gazed fixedly into midair and changed the subject. Margaret Goodwin, née Fraser, was of Edinburgh stock.

The four youngish, tanned, short-haired oilmen were all of Texan stock and had been strangers when they boarded. To the concealed joy of the young Englishman seated opposite Dame Ruth Dean and ostensibly magnetised by the speeding landscape, the Yanks had reached first or nicknames before Friern Barnet and by the Peterborough to Grantham stretch had dealt succinctly with the problems of pipelines, rig supply vessels, rig catering, handling the goddam Brits, Krauts, French, Norwegians, that tough little bunch way up on Shetland, and shifting the wife and kids way over to good old Aberdeen. They were now into their mutual preference for railroad transportation when the goddam pressure was off. 'Sure as hell is the one airport same as the other world-widewise.'

'Ain't that the living truth, Chuck!'

As always when his mental tape-recorder was switched on, Dave Oliver's amused brown eyes looked half asleep. He was a slight, very thin young man with a pale, narrow, over-sensitive face and prematurely grey hair that was long by the neighbouring oilmen's standards but not by those that had obtained when he graduated from Cambridge ten years ago. His good second in Modern Languages had been little help during his subsequent three years as a trainee journalist on first a provincial weekly and then on an evening paper, but had come in useful on his Euro-hols – if not, there and elsewhere, as useful as his ears and memory. He was glad he had decided to use and not flog the ticket and reservation he'd collected in last night's poker. First straight flush of his life! Into a winning streak, mate, he'd told himself; follow it up! Bloody right. He could work this bit alone into a five-minute radio spot. Come on you guys, speak up! I haven't Spock's lugs.

'Is that right, Dix? You have not yet made Hogmanay up in good old Aberdeen? Now hear this. Last year it was seven of the forenoon New Year's Day before Betsy and I got right back home to the kids. The sitter had moved in for the night and was right back on the job that evening and when we got ourselves back to the neighbours' on-going party the folks were kind of surprised we had needed to take the break and we guessed reckoned the enemy aliens real soft, though they did not say so being real neighbourly. Just you make real sure you have plenty ice in the ice-box, Dix. Sure as hell will your head require it.'

'Ain't that the living truth, Chuck!'

Dame Ruth Dean paid no attention to the quiet drawling voices and left her new paperback edition of an old Agatha Christie unopened on the table top. She sat comfortably straight-backed in her seat with her well-tended hands lightly folded in her lap. A good nurse cared for her hands. Dame Ruth Dean had spent forty-one years in the nursing profession and her hands looked twenty years younger than her face that only very recently had looked older than sixty, her present age. She was well aware that the cause was more than a lifetime's neglect of face cream – but it was no use flapping. Flapping never did anything any good. She'd have a quiet word with Mack in Edinburgh – and how nice to see him and Catherine again, and that the boy was having such a good sleep. Only she would have to be careful not to let Jason know she still thought of him as a boy. The dignity of young registrars was so easily ruffled, though they were nothing like as touchy as the consultants. Consultants were even touchier than union officials – though, actually, she'd never had any trouble with any of them. Possibly, she mused with a rare flash of self-insight, that was because she had never anticipated trouble.

So amusing to find Jason just behind her, and as well he was snoozing. Now that he and her three other god-children had grown up, she never quite knew what to say to them. Different when they were small, especially with Jason. He'd really been a jolly little fellow and they'd had great fun together when she'd stayed with his parents. She'd taken him to the zoo, the waxwork and science museums and whenever she had been up during the Festival they'd had ice-creams in the Princes Street Gardens. She'd never eaten an ice-cream in a public garden with anyone else and actually it had been great fun! Such a pity Mack and Catherine couldn't have had more, but in view of Catherine's obstetrical history they'd been very wise.

She was so pleased she had been able to save them the double journey to Waverley station this evening. '15.45 extra if possible,' she told the clerk. 'I've just heard my friends' son should be on that. So much more convenient if you can find me a seat. Any hope?'

'One moment, please, madam – you're in luck! Just one left – but it's a first smoker. That do?'

She had only hesitated momentarily and purely from a habit formed mainly as an example to others. In her long career she had nursed and seen die of carcinoma of the lung too many lifelong nonsmokers whose lives had been spent amongst similar abstainers, to have feared the consequences of nicotine smoke on her own health, had she been capable of the emotion of fear. And having, in her professional youth and prime, been accustomed to the clouds of that smoke wafting from every male ward and down every hospital corridor, and the sight of the medical staff's half-smoked cigarettes stubbed out in heaps in every fire sand bucket outside every ward, she retained a secret nostalgic affection for the smell of stale cigarette smoke and ash.

Yes. A quiet word with Mack. She had every confidence in Professor Donkin and appreciated why he had wanted to take her straight in one of his Martha's beds, but she was relieved he had agreed that her taking this short holiday first might well prove beneficial. Such a nice sound man, only – not Mack. She wanted Mack's opinion on

Professor Donkin first. Mack might have retired but his ear was still very close to the ground and there was no surgeon whose advice she trusted more. She wasn't surprised he'd done so well. She'd foreseen this right back in the war – as had all who worked with him in those rather trying years. Such a pity he left for Edinburgh – but he was a Scotsman – and Jason had come back and if not in his father's class – who could be? – from all reports the boy was doing quite nicely.

Dame Ruth Dean smiled affectionately at the thought of father and son, but neither then nor at any other time in Jason MacDonald's life did it occur to her to remember that once he might have been her son.

The gentle rhythm of the well-sprung train was pleasantly soporific and her calm eyes were uncharacteristically attracted by the swiftly changing view. Her interests normally lay in people, not places and to her 'people' were patients, past, present, or potential. She wasn't too happy about the pallor of the young man opposite. He clearly had some form of anaemia – so mild, fortunately, that it could merely be the consequence of an improper diet – but whatever the cause, he needed more iron. She had recognised this shortly after the train started, but as she had a limited imagination, she had not recognised that owing to her concern for his blood, she had heard he was paying his first visit to Scotland, at the instigation, he said, of his Features Editor.

'Right sadist, that guy: "Never crossed the Border? Don't speak the language? Can't stomach whisky? Right, lad," he says, "get up there for this Hogmanay." ' Dave Oliver invented with such conviction that he temporarily convinced himself and grimaced at his mental picture of the mythical Features Editor bawling him out of his cramped, chaotic, smoke-filled, copy-skied, dummy-pinned-up office. Dave Oliver never admitted he was a freelance to strangers. Say that to most and they equated it with layabout. They should try it. Just one basic rule for freelances – if you don't work you don't eat. He'd done all right since going freelance a couple of years ago – on and off, with more than a little help from poker and the added bonus of looking permanently short on sleep. Nothing opened them up more than the sight of the audience settling down for a good kip. Not that he reckoned anything would get this old bird to open up unless she so decided. And she would 'so decide'. He had her taped as an ex-Head of some classy girls' school in the private sector. 'Onward Christian Soldiers' to open the lungs in morning assembly; 'English Country Gardens' to march the girls out. Girls, not gels. Upper class as hell and no need for pseud affectations. God was in his heaven and all was right with her world and she knew God was an Englishman, and was too old and had seen too much even if she hadn't caught on to what it was all about to waste sweat that God wasn't an Englishwoman. A pleasantly restful old bird to be lumbered with in a train as she was no keener on keeping up the bright chatter than himself. But hell of a waste that he hadn't drawn the seat opposite the blonde with the eyes – he tilted himself sideways in the aisle – or was it? Not sure – though her eyes were worth the in-depth. The big guy sleeping it off didn't know what he was missing – or could be he wouldn't care. Could be the wife was waiting to make with the big welcome home. Dave Oliver's pale thin face suddenly tightened as if it had been slapped and he turned sharply to his window.

Dame Ruth approved of his silence. She hadn't minded exchanging a few words with him as he had been quite amusing and did need iron boosters, but she was not in the habit of talking to strangers on trains. It wasn't that she was unfriendly, but simply that she was English and it just wasn't done.

She hadn't realised Lincolnshire had had so much rain recently. All those pale stretches of water fringed by dark trees and lying so still under the darkening sky were actually rather impressive. The country roads were only marked by pale blurred headlights of the crawling, splashing traffic. The telegraph poles were transformed by the train's speed into tall, frail, finely-linked fences rising forlornly from the false, flat, inland sea. Gracious me! Inches of rain! And then the lights of a distant industrial town made the false sea shimmer; and as the train sped closer, the lighted highrise blocks looked like functioning computers, the high factory chimneys looked like black arms outstretched to the low sky, and the crimson streetlights looked like blobs of venous blood.

Dame Ruth gave herself a mental shake. Absurd to start being fanciful at her age. Things were only what they were; no more, and no less.

'Say, Chuck, would that be a swollen canal or small river?'

'You have me there, Al. Sure as hell running fast as a river.'

Dave Oliver grinned at the Texans. 'Sorry, guys. Stranger to these parts meself.'

Dame Ruth hesitated before turning with dignity and in the voice she used for 'You may sit down, nurses,' announced, 'It's a canal, gentlemen,' and then turned back to her window to demonstrate that her desire to extend courtesy to visitors to her country did not include the wish to be drawn into their conversation.

The Americans chorused, 'Thank you, ma'am,' and exchanged grins and horror stories of the burst canals and rivers encountered on their travels world-wide. Dave Oliver looked at the averted greying-brown head, wondered what he had and the Yanks lacked, and then again leant into the aisle. No rings on the blonde with the eyes. So? His wife had only started wearing hers after the divorce. Found it cut out a lot of sweat, she said.

'Tickets, please . . .'

'Say, guard, there was none of this water when I came right on down Saturday. When'd it fall?'

'Yesterday, mostly, sir.' The West Indian voice was deeply musical. 'When we picked them up in York this morning they were saying the river was over their back gardens and they couldn't get out of their back doors. You'll see some water when we reach York, sir.'

'Is that so? How long?'

'Twenty minutes. Running to time.'

Twenty minutes later, up and down that carriage, up and down the long train it was generally agreed that York looked about to be washed away and if there was one certainty in life it was that it would still be raining in Durham. The emptied seats of the York-bound were promptly filled by the standers from London. The majority of the oncomers were workers returning home to Newcastle and the boarders from King's Cross looked upon them with the resigned contempt of established martyrs for belated and transitory volunteers for the grill, and took a masochistic comfort from the reflection that it was always Newcastle that divided the travellers from the mere commuters.

The landscape began to dry; the first flakes of ice appeared on the few remaining shallow pools; and the short late December afternoon vanished into an early evening that was dark as midnight. And Dave Oliver suddenly caught his breath at the unexpected beauty of a floodlit castle and shadowy cathedral poised over a great carpet of green, orange and white jewels, and backed by a black sea that was just fractionally lighter than the black sky. 'Durham?'

Dame Ruth nodded gracefully. 'We don't stop there – and it's not raining. Must be too cold,' she added with a hint of dismay.

The inference was as lost to Dave Oliver as the magical scene a few seconds later. Then once more the gentle pressure on the brakes made his ears pop and ahead lay an even greater carpet of jewels. 'Newcastle?' he queried just as the West Indian voice made that announcement over the public address system. He slapped his forehead. 'Hollow. Clean forgot they chat us up before stops, but they're slipping. The pilot hasn't told us his name, how high we're flying, what the weather's like on the ground, or that he'll break into manly sobs if we don't all promise to fly with him again.'

Dame Ruth smiled. It did the patients so much good to make little jokes and take an interest in their surroundings and she had always encouraged this. 'It's a pity it'll be too dark for you to see the Tyne when we crawl over the high bridge, so look east. That'll be your best view at this hour. And if you come down in daylight, just before you leave Newcastle station look quickly to your left and you'll just glimpse the ruins of William the Conqueror's castle that gave the city its name.'

'Thanks very much.' Dave tapped one side of his nose with a nicotine-stained forefinger. 'Fancy a good castle, I do.'

'Only ruins, I'm afraid, though not one of those that Cromwell knocked about a bit,' she added brightly. That always tickled the patients.

And that had the Lower Fourth falling out of their desks, thought Dave, smiling as if hearing it for the first time. The old bird was all right. And from her expensively dowdy gear and lack of rings – and no act there for her generation – she'd done more than all right for herself and he had to hand it to her. She was the only aged career woman he'd come across that was neither butch nor bitch. Tough – as an old boot. Bitch – no.

The listening oilmen were amused. Sometime they'd take the look at this real old castle and it sure as hell was kind of cute to keep on calling 'new' a joint that had been around the nine hundred odd years and so forth.

After Newcastle all the remaining standers found seats and as the lights of the city's outskirts vanished a new atmosphere filtered the length of the crowded train. The next stop was Berwick-upon-Tweed and even although partially on English soil, for the overwhelming majority of the passengers it was the first 'home' stop. Strangers exchanged smiles and confidences with strangers temporarily transformed into neighbours, and if some were less desirable than others that was only to be expected since neighbours, like in-laws, were burdens to be borne if possible with pleasure, and if not with the remembrance that there was nae sa bad they couldn'a be worse.

The empty, gently rolling Northumbrian countryside was hidden in the darkness that was sliced by the speeding arrow of light, when one of the Texans stubbed out a cigarette. 'Say, you guys, seeing we have to make the change in Edinburgh and they said back in London there would be the diner on the Aberdeen transport if it is okay with you I guess I'll catch me a bit of shut-eye.'

'Real good thinking, Dix.'

'Ain't that the living truth, Chuck!' reiterated the youngish oilman his companions called Al, for the last time in his life.

2

Lady MacDonald wove a determined, if interrupted path through the assembled company in search of a seat. The occasion, the annual Christmas party of the favourite charity of her old friend and near neighbour Helen Cameron, had drawn a larger crowd than previously by switching its date to just after instead of just before Christmas. There were none of the former lonely pools of light under the first and last of the five ornate chandeliers hanging in line from the high ceiling of the hired reception room. This had once been a private ballroom and still echoed its former Georgian glories in its chandeliers, elegant proportions, exquisite Adam fireplace, and imposingly large double doors to the front hall. But every satin-padded chair and wall settle had been removed and the window-ledges that would have provided perches were hidden behind long golden velvet curtains.

It must be a spinoff from Calvin, thought Lady MacDonald, born Catherine Carter in an East Anglian country vicarage. Festive occasion notwithstanding, let us remember life is not meant for pleasure, man is here to mourn, and all seats out. And if I don't get off these damned heels soon, I'll pass out – and then God help me. The only medics present are young enough to be here for the free booze. Much as I adore our son, Heaven forefend that his lot should lay healing hands on me. They start shoving in tubes and drips, hitching up monitors, and programming computers for diagnoses before they think of laying a finger on a pulse. Just a faint? Far too simple. Obviously a CA (Cardiac Arrest). They'll have George on a mercy dash to intensive care in the Murrayfield before I've surfaced and that won't do his or anyone else's blood-pressure too much good.

'Catherine, how nice to see you – and looking your usual decorative self . . . no George? Busy on the proofs of the reprint? I'm not surprised. My Alistair says your good man's textbook has become the young general surgeons' bible . . .'

'Ah, Lady MacDonald! Looking forward to your laddie's return, I've no doubt . . . indeed, yes, thank you. A most pleasant Christmas with my young folk and they do appear to enjoy staying in that Conglomeration on the Clyde – not that I've ever found the Glaswegians other than the most warm-hearted and hospitable of people, but what they are doing to their – well, I presume I have to term it their city . . . Sir George not with you? Oh, dear – but how understandable . . .'

'There you are, Lady MacDonald! Being such a wee, slender creature you're lost in this crowd . . . Did you hear we made five hundred pounds in our church sale? In just the one morning! And they say there's no money about! May I count on you for your help again with my summer stall? . . . Just let me jot it down in my wee book . . . And where's the Professor? Och, forgive me but having once had the privilege of being his patient he remains the Professor to me . . . what a shame! But when did the Professor not put duty first?'

Sapphira, thought Catherine MacDonald, that's me. Fully paid-up, card-carrying Sapphira. On her husband's admission, to join tonight's gathering he needed to be convinced the gun at his head was loaded, and safety-catch off. 'Unless you really want me along,' he added in another tone. She laughed, kissed him, and left him watching with sardonic amusement a much-repeated Second World War movie on television that at its first showing had reduced them both to hysterical laughter, since, aside from the uniforms, it bore no points of reference to the war that had spent six years of their youth.

Catherine MacDonald was fifty-nine, slight and elegant, with short silvery-grey hair and a lovely fragile face illuminated by expressive dark blue eyes that still turned strange male heads. But she had noticed with the silent laughter that is based in long experience, that all the turning heads now were grey, white, bald, or balding.

'Lady MacDonald, may I not tempt you to a top-up?'

The grey head bowed gallantly. 'Sir George is indeed a brave man to allow his charming wife to venture forth alone. How are you getting home? May I not have the pleasure . . . och, collecting you on his way to Waverley. I can but hope he'll find a parking space. When I drove along this afternoon to uplift my son and daughter-in-law and the children, I'd to drive in and out the three times before I could squeeze in . . .'

'Jason and your friend the Dame coming up on the 3.45, Catherine? I thought the 125s left London on the hour . . . oh, an extra. No doubt we should be grateful British Rail have realised we Scots have this weakness for returning to our homeland for Hogmanay. So often in the past I've had the impression they've been as oblivious to the fact that the year ends on the 31st of December as to the fact that Edinburgh has an annual Festival and –'

'Must you remind us of the Festival, Fiona! I declare we have not yet recovered from the last. Naturally, we ignored it. Personally, I hope that if we all continue to ignore it long enough it will eventually have the decency to get up quietly and go away. My dear Catherine, you'll not credit what occurred to us this year. We even had some people from the Fringe seeking to hire our wee hall. Naturally, Hamish was adamant. What may transpire elsewhere, said Hamish, does not necessarily have to obtain to the property entrusted to my care . . . oh, yes, Fiona! We were aware that this year even in Murrayfield – but as Hamish said, someone must draw the line somewhere.'

Catherine assumed an apologetic air on behalf of herself, her husband and fellow-residents of the Murrayfield district of Edinburgh, changed the subject to the success of the church sale, shifted from one high heel to the other, and thought, My God, the things I do for Scotland.

'Do try a cheesy one, Lady MacDonald. Positively delish! Or does cheese upset you at night?' The tall, shapely, vacuously pretty brunette offering the dish of homemade canapés consciously packed the caring note into her high, clear, English voice. 'How about anchovies? Or a mushroom vol-au-vent? Stacked with mushrooms. I know. I stacked them.'

'Thanks, Gill, but I like cheese', said Catherine with the gently blank smile that in her youth had convinced the mentally myopic that she was a typically dumb chocolate-box blonde. 'Helen's told me your help's been invaluable.'

Gill Cameron, the wife of the second of Helen and Donald Cameron's three sons, accepted the smile and compliment with satisfaction and contempt. These fading female anachronisms that had been content to spend their useless, sheltered lives in their husband's shadows were pushovers. All you had to do was smarm. Lady M., as the in-laws and all their friends, was positively prehistory. He hadn't had to warn her last night Edinburgh wasn't London. More than worlds apart – half a century. She had thought Wales needed to be dragged screaming out of the dark, dank 1930s, but after those two weeks last summer and these last ten days in her in-laws' Edinburgh – the 1930s were in the distant future. Their lives and attitudes reminded her exactly of her grandmother's descriptions of her pre-1914 youth in London. And yet, if she hadn't let Paul drag her and the kids up for the last Festival she wouldn't have met Jason. She had to see him again – soon. She couldn't wait till he got back to London. Not after that trauma the last time – but how could she have known he really was working? It was supposed to be his free afternoon.

Gill Cameron was thirty, but the roundness of her face and the short curls attractively covering her whole head, made her look younger. She wore a tight-fitting purple velvet dress with a one-sided slit skirt and deep square neckline that enhanced the creamy quality of her skin, and the lines of her bosom that were as beautiful as her long legs. She looked lovely, thought Catherine, and a very hot little number. And her mind went back to one evening early last September when Jason, home for the final week of the Festival, had belatedly met his old schoolfriend Paul Cameron's wife, having had to miss their wedding nine years ago owing to a mild attack of glandular fever. The meeting had taken place in the MacDonalds' drawing room and after watching it Jason's parents had exchanged a long look.

'Paul baby-sitting?'

'No alternative for the poor sweet. Mother C.'s help couldn't manage tonight as well as tomorrow and I had to lend the odd hand here. Not that Paul minds. He's super with the kids!'

Catherine made the expected enquiries about the children and avoided the subject of the young family's move to London last September. Paul Cameron, a large, plain amicable civil servant, had been transferred from Glasgow to Wales after his marriage to a fellow graduate of his English redbrick university whom he had first met when he was a third and she a first year. Gill had married a few weeks after taking a second in English Literature. They had remained in Wales until the recent move to London. Paul's a sweet lad, thought Catherine, but too honest and unimaginative to suspect or accept dishonesty in others until the evidence is presented to him in writing and in triplicate.

Gill talked on, '. . . so we just had to opt out of our London plans and stay up. It's years since the whole family was under one roof at New Year. Paul's younger brother, wife and the new baby are due from Fort William for lunch tomorrow, Dick and family are driving in from West Linton for tea and Mother C.'s over the moon!'

'So I've gathered,' replied Catherine truthfully. Paul was very much his mother's son. From last September, at regular intervals, Helen Cameron had decorously enthused to Catherine over the renewal of the boys' old friendship, the relative proximity of Islington to St Martha's, and the good fortune contained in Jason's irregular hours that allowed him to call over and cheer up poor Gill, who was understandably a wee bit lonely knowing so few people in London and being tied down to the flat, to ferrying the wee ones to and from nursery and primary school, and with the added disadvantage that Paul's work frequently necessitated his staying on to attend late evening meetings.

This morning in their local baker's shop Helen Cameron had admitted herself really touched by Gill's insistence on sacrificing two parties in London to keep the family together in Edinburgh. On repeating this to her husband, Catherine added, 'I had to say they must come with the others to our party tomorrow.'

Professor Sir George MacDonald nodded noncommittally and they had exchanged a look identical to the one in their drawing room on that particular evening in last September. Their love for each other went so deep and their accord was so close that throughout their marriage, that was the second for both, in public or private they could communicate instantly, unspokenly, on any turn of events. For Catherine only, a very similar relationship had obtained in her first marriage, ended in 1951 by her husband's death from pulmonary tuberculosis at thirty-one. George MacDonald's first wife had been only twenty-eight when their short, childless and disastrously incompatible marriage had been ended with her being killed outright by a shot-down VI flying-bomb. Catherine had been Gill Cameron's present age when she married quietly in Edinburgh the then youngish Professor MacDonald in the first week of January, 1953. Jason, a honeymoon baby, had been born and Catherine had very nearly died, two days before the Christmas of that year.

He's got my father's height and build, my eyes, forehead and nose, thought Catherine, but George's hair, jaw, voice, and devastating sexuality, so it's not surprising that, like George at his age, he hasn't yet worked out that eventually you have to get out of bed and start talking. Or has he just begun to catch on to that and to remember Paul, those two little kids, and that he has to look at his face when he shaves? Something's wrong. Something's worrying her so much she wants me as her buddy-girl. Tough luck, duckie. I'm not that dumb and make no apologies for disliking a situation for which I chiefly blame my son. I wouldn't give a damn if you were single, but you aren't and no one ever told me Paul needed a shotgun to get you to the altar or to bear his first or second child. So what if there's a lot of it about? Lot of road accidents about – and children emotionally crippled for life by their parents' divorces. Different were Paul a swine, but he's not. Good husband, good father, good provider whom you, academically educated, free and C. of E. chose to marry – fine. So you don't think having a paramour matters? Right. Your privilege. Mine, not to like it.

Gill was still talking, '. . . such a super idea kicking off with an English New Year's Eve party before the Scottish Hogmanay gets off the ground. Father C. says makes very useful ballast from midnight onwards – we're all going first-footing. I've never first-footed – can't wait! Of course we had parties in Wales – if you could call them parties – total segregation of the sexes – and we always had them at home – I say! Didn't – er – didn't Mother C. tell me you were raised in a Norfolk vicarage? Daddy's is in wildest Hampshire – of course you came to our wedding and poor Jason couldn't – haven't we a lot in common!'

Catherine held up one agonised high-heeled foot. 'Do you have my fenwoman's webbed toes?'

Gill threw back her head laughing and the gesture and her height enabled her to see over the crowd the tallish, spare, white-haired man in a tweed overcoat impassively surveying the room from the open double doorway. 'Here's Sir George! What a pity! Must you leave so soon?'

'George, already?' Catherine glanced at her watch in concealed relief that was only slightly evaporated by the discovery that he was much too early. The movie wouldn't have gripped him and he knew she was longing to be rescued. 'I can't see through this crowd. Give him a wave to show I'm on my way, please, Gill. Do forgive me. See you all tomorrow night and my love to Paul and –' Her voice stopped abruptly. Gill was too happy waving and thinking her own thoughts to notice. But just then the crowd had parted sufficiently for husband and wife to see each other. They were about thirty feet apart and both had good eyesight.

Catherine maintained an outward smiling composure whilst she made her way and farewells through the assembly, but when she reached the doorway the face she raised had frozen to a blank mask. 'Jason?' she mouthed.

No flicker of emotion disturbed the thin, lined clever face to which age had added distinction and from which years of marital happiness had erased the former harshness. 'I don't know, dearest.' Sir George MacDonald kept the pain out of his voice but not from the back of his dark eyes. 'I don't bloody know yet. No one does.' He took her arm, walked her into the wide front hall and amongst the swirls of cigarette and cheroot smoke and echoes of voices and laughter, told her precisely why he had come early. Then, 'I wanted you to hear it from me. The news flash will have it all round, shortly. Nothing we can do, pro tem, but wait. Let's get home to the phone. The police have our number.'

Catherine felt icy cold and beyond speech, then heard her voice saying quietly, 'I'll just get my coat, my darling.'

3

They had it right, Catherine thought numbly. All those relatives of air raid victims in the war, had it exactly right . . . 'You know as it's happening all the time, nurse, but you keeps thinking – can't happen to me – then it does and there's nothing as you can do but stand there feeling like your guts been kicked out leaving you hollow and helpless, like. That's when you starts praying, nurse, even if you've not said the one since you was a nipper – and it's the happening sudden, nurse, what has you all of a tremble – that'll be what you calls the shock, isn't it, nurse? Not that I'm saying it's not as bad when it happens slow, but different bad. When it's slow you got a bit of time to take it in – to face as you got to get used to going back home and seeing the empty chair – but when it's sudden and you got the dinner cooking as'll not be wanted – different.'

Hundreds of times in the war; scores of times in the peace, after road accidents . . . 'You knows as it's happening all the time, staff nurse' . . . 'You know as it's happening all the time, sister' . . . 'it's the suddenness, like – not saying it isn't as bad but different, like, when it happens slow . . .'

Yes. Different when it happened slowly and you happened to be a young trained nurse and had recognised the fatal symptoms before . . . 'I deeply regret having to tell you this, Mrs Jason, but I am afraid Dr Jason's lungs are already beyond eventual recovery . . . you'll understand I can't be too specific . . . possibly a year or two – possibly longer . . . oh yes, I agree! He has enough to carry without this and whilst, most regrettably, hope cannot cure him, it will help him greatly, though the strain of concealing the truth from him must, I fear, add as greatly to your own burden . . . yes, I'm sure you will manage – and I am so very sorry . . .'

Three years for getting used to the empty chair, to turning, half-awake, in bed, and finding yourself alone. Then: 'Couldn't have been kinder, Mrs Jason. He died in sleep and hope.'

Very different, in some respects. Not others. Both young men, Martha's men, just coming up to their prime. One her deeply loved and loving young husband; one the son she loved beyond measure.

George MacDonald glanced at her as they stood by Jason's intensive therapy bed, and saw the look in her eyes above her loaned white disposable face mask, and thought with pain of new pain's habit of awaking old pain, and then returned his guarded gaze to the enlarged screen of the bedside cardiac monitor.

The spacious intensive therapy cubicle was as clean and hot as an operating theatre and had the same impersonal atmosphere; the same constant, quiet, well-ordered activity of the staff. But in place of a theatre team, were the four especially trained staff nurses on-duty that morning, and, as the small resident staff, they moved continuously in and out of the three cubicles in a row that were the hospital's only Intensive Therapy Unit. The small hospital was the Holydale General and the only one in the little Northumbrian country town of that name.

The faint humming and ticking of the air-conditioner, and the battery of medical machines, and the still figure in a shock-, anaesthetic-, and drug-induced coma on the brilliantly constructed IT bed, enhanced the similarity to a theatre. The figure was naked, with, instead of sterile theatre towels, a single loose sheet draped from waist to high thigh to expose the new plasters, one enveloping the right shoulder and arm to the knuckles, another the right leg from mid-thigh to just-exposed toes; the new strapping round the ribs; the web of rubber and transparent tubes. Some tubes were connected to the machines; others reached up to the overhanging transfusion and infusion stands. In the shadowless lighting, the transparent bags sparkled redly and whitely, and bulged like hideous fruit hanging from white, leafless, surrealistic trees with long, obscene red and white tentacles, reaching down and growing into the uninjured left arm and leg temporarily immobilised in back-splints. And against the white pillows, the young black hair was dull, lifeless; and under the transparent oxygen mask the clarity of the strong, regular bone structure was blurred by swelling, purple, black and brown bruises and innumerable grazes and scratches. But the eyes, skull, brain, and spinal cord were undamaged and so was the strong young heart.

George MacDonald, his eyes on the cardiac monitor, stooped to breathe in Catherine's ear 'His heart's taking it.'

She nodded numbly. Her forehead was white as her mask and loaned long-sleeved, theatre-type gown. She glanced left then right through the two-third glass walls dividing the cubicles. Jason was in 2. Three theatres in a row going at once she thought, then corrected it. Not theatres; battery cells; not for chickens for killing; for humans for saving – but still battery cells. And then she thought, thank God this little place has them.

It had been after midnight before they heard Jason was alive. By then the quiet of the midwinter night had settled over residential Murrayfield and the lights of the hospital that sprawled along the crest of the long, lowish hill had shone out over the solid grey roofs and unlighted glass cupolas ranged in tiers running up from the long, wide Corstorphine Road that was part of the main Edinburgh–Glasgow route. In the houses and flats most of the fairy lights in the Christmas trees in front windows had been switched off, but a few still glittered in darkened rooms with the windows left uncurtained whilst the trees were in place. Only a few bedroom lights remained on behind closed curtains and outside, in the cold night air, the streetlights, large and yellow as radioactive plums, hung over the quiet pavements, the occasional dark streaks of cats, and silent ranks of cars parked outside their owners' homes in the near-silent roads running up and across the long, lowish hill. Just westwards, the higher, green Corstorphine Hill was a black shadow; the invisible Forth to the north, just a hint of salt in the cold air; and on the southern horizon, the rolling dark outlines of the Pentland Hills were patched with white.

They waited in George's study, their family sanctuary on the ground floor at the back of their house that was one of the few detached in their road. It had been built at the turn of the century, tallish, squarish, solid and grey and though not much more than five hundred yards above the main Edinburgh–Glasgow road, no sound of the perpetual heavy night traffic penetrated the thick stone walls, double-glazing and thick crimson study curtains. We could be the only people in a silent world – always the way of it, thought George MacDonald. Anxiety of this nature cuts out the rest of humanity as if it has encapsulated the anxious in opaque glass.

He glanced, as he kept glancing, at the silent lighted screen of the portable television he had brought down from Jason's bedroom when they got home. The sound was turned down until the next news flash or bulletin. He watched Catherine in her usual study chair and his mind returned, as it had kept returning, to the first Christmas after their marriage when he had spent two days and nights at her hospital bedside before coming home alone on Christmas night. 'Away with you, man. Get some sleep,' said Professor Obstetrics. 'Now she knows she's a healthy son, she'll do. Go home and sleep.' He had come home to the empty house, gone straight to his study, sat at his desk, stared at Catherine's empty chair, and wept. Waiting and watching her now, watching her age years for every hour of waiting, he could have wept had he not been too old for tears other than those of relief. There was no relief for him in that waiting. He had seen too often, treated too often, been incapable of treating too often, the consequences of human folly, human thoughtlessness and man's inhumanity to man, for the relief of false hopes and his head had never allowed him the relief of prayer. He had learnt to respect and love in Catherine the white-hot faith in her very personal God that neither war nor great grief had been able to dim. He knew she had been praying mentally since they left the reception and was grateful she had that comfort. In his agony for her and the life of his beloved son, his heart fought his head and nearly forced from his lips the ageless heart-cry of the agnostic – 'If You do exist – for Christ's sake – please – help!'

Just after midnight, they heard Jason had been one of the few brought out alive from the second carriage, the only one to have swung broadside down when the engine leapt the vandalised track dragging behind it, upright, the first carriage. All those behind the second had jumped to the opposite side of the track and run on, upright and unentangled, until the line stopped of its own accord in the shelter of a highish fold in the moors that hid the lights of an isolated village roughly one mile back and five miles from Holydale.

Forty minutes later, as promised, he rang Donald Cameron. After their first exchange, Donald Cameron said, 'Helen says to tell you we'll attend to everything up here. I'll be round for your spare keys in a few minutes. I'll be ringing you at The Swan, Holydale, tomorrow evening.'

They had been very kind at the hotel, thought Catherine, though she couldn't remember whom 'they' were, or anything else about the hotel. She couldn't remember what the hospital looked like; only the smell when they walked into the main reception hall as it had been the ubiquitous hospital smell of floor polish, anaesthetics, antiseptics, and warm, overused air. But so many differences in here and the greatest of all was the way, with one exception, every member of the staff she had yet seen in this cubicle, watched the machines and not the patient. Always in the theatre in her own and in George's time, the patient had been the chief focus of eyes and attention.

The exception was a tall, willowy redhaired staff nurse with a smooth high white forehead and grave green eyes above her white mask. It was with a surge of gratitude that Catherine watched the girl give Jason's uninjured left shoulder a gentle pat after rechecking the position of his cardiac electrodes. She's the only person we've met here so far, thought Catherine, who seems aware he's an injured young human being and our adored son.

They had been met in the front hall by a short chubby young woman house officer with a flaxen fringe, crumpled white coat, and brusque manner. 'Dr MacDonald's parents? Yes, Mr Benson has said you may see him – yes, Mr Benson is our consultant orthopaedic surgeon – no, you can't see him. In theatre. How's he doing? Satisfactory . . . Miss Dean? . . . Oh, Dame Ruth Dean – are you relatives? Well, I can tell you she's been admitted and is comfortable – oh no, you can't see her – only close relatives –

this way.' She marched ahead up some stairs.

Same stairs. Old, cold and stone – but how many? One flight? Several? Catherine didn't notice. Only from long-conditioned and forgotten old habit did she automatically notice the name Surgical A Ward on a large board, and on a smaller beneath and in capitals INTENSIVE THERAPY UNIT. NO UNAUTHORISED VISITORS. Then they were through double swing glass doors and into an egg-shell-blue spaceage world. She didn't recognise the long blue fibreglass counter as the sister's desk, nor that it was set to face across a spacious alcove the line of cubicles and had bay wards running from its immediate left and right. But again her old training forced her to register that whilst the large fair young woman in a sister's uniform behind the blue counter nodded pleasantly at them, she did not come forward to speak to them.

'In here.' The house officer opened the glass door in the glass front wall of the cubicle. 'Stand over there on the right. Only a few minutes. Mr Benson doesn't want his patient disturbed.'

George MacDonald, without taking his gaze from his son, said, 'Just one minute please, doctor.' He reached under his gown for the wallet in his breast pocket and took out one of his seldom used visiting cards. 'Would you be good enough to hand this to Mr Benson when he's free and ask if he can kindly spare me a few minutes.'

'All right, but he probably won't have time today. We're very busy.' She thrust the card in her white coat top pocket without looking at it, but neither of Jason's parents noticed or saw her leave.

A hand lightly touched Catherine's shoulder. 'Wouldn't you care for a wee sit down, Mrs MacDonald?' The red-haired staff nurse tipped her paper-capped head at the blue high stool she had placed behind Catherine. 'Standing about gets awful tiring.'

'Thank you, nurse – oh sorry –' Catherine read the name label pinned to the girl's gown 'Staff Nurse Hogg'.

'No bother. You should hear the names I get called.' Staff Nurse Hogg spoke in a cheerful murmur and her green eyes moved to and from Jason and the machines. 'Don't fret too much that your son looks out for the count. That's mostly the drugs. He's doing just fine.' She moved off too swiftly for Catherine to answer, then returned with another high stool. 'One for you, Mr MacDonald.'

Old conditioning to that address from a nurse jerked his head round and for the first time in hours his eyes smiled quickly. 'Thanks, Staff, I'd rather stand.'

Staff Nurse Hogg's eyes returned the smile. 'Suit yourself,' she retorted equably, put away the stool and returning to the machines and her colleague murmured something that made the shorter, stockier girl's forehead redden.

They're all so terrifyingly young, thought Catherine, but that's the same. It was always the newly trained young nurses that did the actual work on the dangerously ill; then as now, the residents – and consultants when we see one – came and went from the wards; the nurses stay put. Only the young have the mental and physical stamina that's as vital as the skill, for withstanding the constant strain of literally holding lives in their hands. Only here – no, not in their hands – in the hands of the machines, they are nursing the machines – not Jason. I think the redhead wants to do more of what I'd call nursing, but she's well trained, they all are, and they've been trained to nurse the machines – as they must. The machines are doing a wonderful, if ahuman job; these girls are operating their complexities with the ease with which a trained nurse of my era shook down a thermometer. Juniors nearly shook their arms off. The trained – just one flick of the wrist – oh God! His right arm. When is someone going to tell us what we want – what we must – what we have every right to know? Oh my darling boy – no, I mustn't! Not for him – not for my darling George – he's in hell too – think of something else, quick! Think – think – why hasn't that little so-and-so come to chuck us out? The redhead doesn't mind us around or she wouldn't have given me this stool and presumably she's the senior on this morning as her partner's just shooting us resigned glances like the other two. Or has someone somewhere now caught on and told them this isn't the first time George has been in a hospital ward? He only gave our name, relationship to Jason, home address and telephone number over the phone last night when they told us the minimum. As this morning. Why hasn't the sister come in? And told us?

Was it minutes, years, or about an hour later that a sister came in? Not the large fair one. A youngish, brown-haired capless woman with small clever eyes above her mask. She ignored Catherine, but said 'Good morning,' to George, looked for some seconds at Jason, and for some minutes at the machines. She talked softly with the red-head, then backed to stand by George. 'Responding and stable,' she said.

'Indeed, sister.'

She nodded and removed herself. Staff Nurse Hogg waited till the glass door closed to move over to Catherine. 'That was one of the Nursing Officers. She's a clinical nurse teacher.'

'In charge of intensive therapy?'

Mary Hogg's eyes were amused. 'That's a good question. She's one of the top brass and they're aye getting under our feet.'

Catherine's eyes smiled in gratitude. 'From Glasgow, Staff?'

'How'd you guess – coming from Edinburgh?' She gently touched one of Catherine's cold hands. 'I wasn't kidding just now to soothe you. Your laddie's a wee bit poorly but he's doing just fine.'

'Thank you very much, Staff.'

'You're welcome – excuse me –' She moved swiftly back to the machines and made some slight adjustment.

Another timeless stretch, then, 'Would you both please come with me?' The large fair sister had donned a mask and gown over her long-sleeved white uniform dress. 'Mr Benson will see the gentleman now. I'll take your wife along to our relatives' rest-room and Dr Meredith will take you to Mr Benson's office.' She gestured to the young woman house officer waiting in the large alcove looking rather pinkfaced and staring at her feet. 'If you'll just give me your gowns outside – thank you. This way, Mrs MacDonald.'

That time Catherine saw that an eight-bedded bay ward ran off from the right of the blue counter, the row of black oxygen cylinders against the right wall running from the ward entrance and on into a broadish long corridor that she later discovered ran parallel with the one containing the stairs and liftwell. The sister opened an eggshell blue door. 'In here, dear. I don't expect your husband will be long.'

'Thank you, sister,' said Catherine mechanically to the already closed door. She sat mechanically in a comfortable, dark blue leather armchair and stared at the outsize cheese plant on a low table by a window that overlooked the staff car park, the narrow, hilly high street and grey buildings of the little town and just glimpsed the rolling sepia moors beyond. She didn't notice the view or how long she waited alone in that smallish, warm, well-furnished rest room. She stared at the cheese plant, and thought, the leaves needed sponging, with the intensity she invariably gave trivialities when under acute stress. And then she had to think of Jason's face in infancy, childhood, teens, manhood – and under that transparent oxygen mask. And she heard his still cracking fifteen-year-old voice, defiant to cover teenage embarrassment, 'I've decided what I want to do, Mum. Surgery, but not like Dad – I'm not that bright. I don't want to do general. I want to be an orthopod.'

'Keep on growing the way you are, darling, and one thing's sure, your build'll be in your favour. Orthopaedic surgeons need strong arms and shoulders more than most. Hey, boy, put me down!'

'Just proving I can now lift you with one arm. Took two first time – but I was only a kid.'

'All of nine, duckie – thanks. And for God's sake turn down the volume before Dad gets home. He says if his eardrums are busted once more with "Love Me Do" he'll do you!'

'Sorry you've had this long wait, Lady MacDonald.' The voice that jolted her back into the present had a very faint Australian accent. 'Didn't know you'd been trained or you could have come in with Sir George. I'm Arthur Benson.'

He was just shorter but twice as wide as George and had the face of an intelligent, mature, badly-shaven cherub and short spiky light brown hair. Only needs a cap with a bell and Big Ears in the background, thought Catherine with the momentary lightheaded irreverence of acute anxiety.

Mr Benson's round tired eyes were self-derisively

amused by his own reaction to that card. Stiffen the bloody lizards, he'd thought. The handle meant bugger-all to him but it wasn't every day a bit of modern surgical history walked into his office and made him feel he was facing his first viva. His old lady was the closest Mr Benson had seen to a living bit of bloody Dresden china. Being in the habit of using the truth when he could, he said, 'Just been telling Sir George I'm glad I didn't know whose son I was patching up last night. Your son's a bit bashed up as you've seen, but with his head intact our main problem's that right arm. Sir George'll give you the details. The right leg's what you'd expect from rapid deceleration – she'll be right in time. Right ribs got a bit cracked but no penetration of the lung. Lacerations are a bit messy – only superficial. Seems a healthy young bloke. Strong. Useful allies,' he allowed laconically.

Catherine dragged her gaze from George's rigid face. 'Yes. Thank you, Mr Benson. I'm afraid you've had a bad night here.'

Mr Benson was forty, had had no sleep since he got up yesterday morning and had never known a worse professional night than this last. 'Stirred the possum a bit, Lady MacDonald. Could've been worse. I hear you've not yet seen today's papers. All calling it a miracle. I could use another word for the – umm – the vandals that set it up. Just a parcel of kids the police reckon. When they get 'em – if they get 'em – probably get probation – that's not my problem. Not that the papers are far wrong if you forget the second carriage. All the others got themselves out – carriages stayed upright and unentangled because of their special construction and couplings the papers say. Could be right. I wouldn't know.' The mature cherubic face darkened with anger but the voice remained mild. 'I do know we had in the only seven that came out of the second alive. We had in a parcel of others with minor injuries. Needed two special coaches to take them away but didn't need more from us than a bit of dusting off, fishing out glass splinters, slapping on a bit of plaster, strapping up a few sprains. Let 'em all go after they'd rested off the shock – wanted to get home – the railway had all that side organised. Hope they've got home all right. Expect so, or someone would have told me.'

Catherine breathed carefully. 'Still just the seven we knew about last night?'

'I'm afraid so. Took a bit of time for the heavy lifting gear and oxyacetylene cutters to clear enough to be sure. Sure now, they tell me.' Mr Benson glanced at Sir George and didn't repeat the description he had given in his office and had had from the medical registrar and the senior house officer who, with two staff nurses – one of these had been Mary Hogg – had been in the first ambulance at the scene of the crash. 'Five adults, two boys. Brothers from what he found on them. Police contacted their parents. We kept the boys in overnight and sent them on to Alanbridge General this morning. Biggest hospital in our district. Takes all the kids. But twenty-three miles northwest from here. We were nearest. The boys are a bit bashed up but should get back to school for the summer term. No cranial damage. Don't ask me why. They were up to the drive this morning and arrived safely, they tell me. We haven't had paediatric wards here since Sir Keith Joseph made a – made a parcel of changes to the NHS in the mid-70s. Shifted all our gynae to Alanbridge then,' he added inconsequentially to Catherine but not, she saw to George. "In luck, those seven. Don't ask me why. Might say they were sitting in the right places for what happened if that hadn't a hole in it.' He pushed a broad, stubby-fingered hand through his hair and caught Sir George's almost imperceptible nod. 'Wife of one of our admissions wasn't in luck but we guess she was sitting with her husband.'

Another ghost haunted Catherine's eyes. 'Poor woman. Poor man. Does he know?'

'Not yet.' Again the men exchanged glances but this time the older gave no nod, and there was a small silence that all three recognised from other times and other places but the same cause.

Mr Benson roused himself. 'Not a young bloke. Name's Halstead. We've got him in the Cells – that's what everyone here calls the IT cubicles. Mr Halstead's in 3, your son in 2, your friend Dame Ruth Dean in 1.'

Catherine's eyes widened in shock. She had glanced frequently into 1 this morning. She had not even been able to recognise the sex of the patient that was Ruth.

'May I ask – how is she?'

'Not too well, I'm afraid.'

She had to look at her lap. She knew how that translated. 'I'm – so – sorry.'

'Early yet, Lady MacDonald. I'm sorry you've not been able to see her but I told Dr Meredith only close relatives or named next-of-kins.'

The figure in 1 had a cranial bandage. 'Brain damage?'

'None. Skull has a hairline crack and she was a bit concussed and had a bit of internal damage and the rapid deceleration injuries to her left leg and lacerations and bruising. I had to go into her abdominal cavity to plug things up, not too bad, but very shocked. Have to expect that as she's not so young. She's been giving the police a bit of a problem. From the contents of the handbag we thought was hers, we put the police onto St Martha's but all they could give was the name of some cousin that's in Canada –'

'David Hartley.'

'That's the name. Sir George has just explained her only relative in this country is an elderly widowed aunt. Sir George rang this aunt from my office and she's asked him to act next-of-kin. Save us a parcel of trouble having Sir George in that capacity. You two are the first of the relatives to reach us. One of Mr Halstead's is arriving from Edinburgh sometime today, but no one's told me if any of Miss Turner's or Mr Oliver's are coming – they're the pair that make up our five. Both young and a bit bashed up but doing right in Bay 1 –' Mr Benson jerked his head at the door. 'Bay 1's the smaller of Surgical A's two wards.' He looked back at the silent, still, rigidly impassive, white-haired man standing by his wife's chair. 'Sir George has just had a look at Dame Ruth Dean. I'd like her to have it quiet for a day or so. You'll not mind waiting till then to see her? Sir George'll be going in and out.'

'Of course not. Thank you very much.'

'She'll be right,' said Mr Benson kindly, not in reference to Dame Ruth Dean, but in general reassurance. 'Hear you've moved into The Swan. Not a bad little place. Good breakfasts. Only three-star but Holydale's a quiet little spot out of season – in summer – oh my word, can't move for visitors up for walking tours over the moors and to look at the Wall. Wall's worth seeing if you like your ruins with a parcel of wind and not much more. Must have been

– umm – mighty cold for all those blokes in their dinkie kilts. Their kidneys must have given Hadrian a bit of a problem. Hope the noise tonight won't give you too much of a problem. Swan's got the only decent ballroom in Holydale in their new annex. Always have a dance New Year's Eve.'

Dear God, thought Catherine, that's what it is. Last night's reception, tonight's party Helen's cancelling for us, Gill – and Jason – don't just seem in another lifetime but too trivial for a moment's reflection. And that hasn't altered either. Nothing anywhere, any time, turns a stronger spotlight on one's real priorities than the light in the valley of the shadow.

4

For the first morning in ten Jason woke before his final blood pressure check of the night that in Surgical A ended officially at 8 a.m., ten minutes after the day nurses came on-duty. He woke with a start and such a strong sensation of having lost something vital that before his eyes opened his left hand reached for the plaster on his right arm. Still there – of course it bloody was. Now he was out of the Cells neither Benson nor anyone else would take it off without his signature on the consent form and if anyone but Benson laid the tip of a knife on it, Benson would feed that person into a meatgrinder.

The dark green glow of Bay 1's night lights gave his arm plaster a pearly sheen and made the beads of fresh sweat on his forehead and upper lip glisten darkly. The rash movement of his left arm and shoulder muscles had sent hot wires of pain down his right arm. He had to wait till the pain subsided to the habitual heavy ache before mopping his face with the blue cotton left sleeve of his pyjama jacket that was one of the many from which his mother had removed the right sleeve, slit open the right underarm seam and right shoulder seam to the collar, after he was moved into Bay 1 five days ago.

He should've remembered the consent form and that last night someone – who? – got it! – Ma Mastin – had told him Benson had gone home to his wife for the first night since the 30th, when she pushed up and plugged in the portable telephone trolley. She'd then left him to take that call from – what in hell was her name? Christ, he was muzzy. Ma Mastin's knockouts seemed to have given his brain-stem nearly as tough a battering as all those muscle relaxants in the Cells. He couldn't remember – her – name – just all that emotional trauma last time in London and in her voice last night. '. . . you don't know what I've been through – just – just don't know! I've kept ringing but they wouldn't put me through – they just wouldn't let me talk to you . . . you know I couldn't leave my name. Surely you could've done something – even a postcard to Paul – you knew I couldn't ring from Edinburgh – you know there are never any boxes working round here . . . yes, of course from home! It's Wednesday! You know Paul always has late meetings on Wednesdays . . . yes, both asleep, at last! I just had to try – you don't know what I've been through – you should've realised! You know I've got this terrif. horror of hospitals and seeing sick people and things – too sensitive, I suppose. You are all right? You sound all right . . .'

Gill. Yes. Gill, he thought, and remembered telling her he was sorry she had been upset, that he was all right, and dreading the moment when she asked about his arm and when that moment had not come been too relieved to be hurt. And when Staff Nurse Mastin, the nurse in charge of both Bay wards last night, had come to remove the portable telephone, she had eyed him sharply. 'Whether you're now allowed calls or not, that's the last you're taking tonight, Dr MacDonald. If Mr Benson were to walk in now he'd have my guts for garters. I'm leaving your curtains closed for a while and coming straight back with sedatives – don't you try that on me, young man! Save that for green lasses. I may be young enough to enjoy your soft-talk but I'm too old to swallow it. You're having the tablets and that's that!'

Jason smiled faintly. Good old Ma Mastin, though her home-life must be a shade dodgy. One born Sergeant-Major and one ex-Master At Arms. She was a handsome piece and a comfortable armful but it figured that old Mastin hadn't objected to her working nights now the kids had left home. This last year had probably been his first in twenty-five when he'd been able to wear his slippers around the house, drink beer out of a can and watch Match of the Day.

The smile vanished. Jason's mind had cleared enough to recall the dream that had woken him. He had been on a train – not *the* – another, with small old-fashioned carriages with doors each side and no corridor. They had had the carriage to themselves, only in the dream she had been backing and he facing the engine, though still he hadn't been able to see her face clearly. They'd been talking – he didn't know what about – when the train suddenly stopped at an unnamed station and she had jumped out slamming the door. He had tried to follow her, but couldn't open the door and when he managed to get down the window and stick his head out she had vanished, the train had restarted and carried him away from that empty nameless station feeling – amputated.

Just association of ideas. Just his subconscious probing into the nightmare his conscious refused to recall – if it had been on the job long enough to record much more. He had a total blackout between the moments when he had woken in the violently swaying darkness and heard the shouts and cries and when, on his second day in the Cells, he had surfaced long enough to know his parents had been around for some time and ask, 'What's under this arm plaster, Dad?'

'From your X-rays, tests, op. notes and Benson's description, a sound job of rebuilding.'

'Was it off?'

'No, or you'd have had to lose it. You'd lost too much blood and were too shocked to have stood the couple of hours or more to the nearest micro-surgery unit, even with fast police escort. Your arm was crushed. Benson had to get straight on with the job.'

He had known his father would tell him the truth. The old man was incapable of lying, even to save his own skin, and this ruthless honesty had made him innumerable professional enemies, but none amongst his patients or their relatives. He hadn't asked the old man more about his arm; he knew what the job of reconnecting bones, blood vessels, muscles, nerves and skin involved. Nor had he asked how much use he might eventually have in that arm; no one knew that answer yet. 'Is Benson the Australian guy?'

'Yes. Benedict's man. Came over to qualify and stayed. His father's a Benedict's man – Englishman – brain-drained to New South Wales in the early '50s, but wanted his son to come back to qualify. Good thing for you and others that he did. Very sound chap.'

'That's useful. Dad – many others get out?'

'Not from your carriage but from the others, the lot. Five from your carriage are still in this hospital, the Holydale General. This is one of the smallest in the Alanbridge health district but, very fortunately, their Surgical A ward that includes this IT unit was totally restructured and re-equipped just before the great NHS shake-up that had just got started before I retired, and the more recent economic clampdown. Equipment here's as good as anything I've seen in the Murrayfield or Martha's. But you've talked enough pro tem, laddie. Ease off a wee while.'

'Right.' He had looked from his father to his mother sitting silently on a high stool and hadn't asked if they were all right. He could see their eyes.

The following morning he had asked the redhaired staff nurse he then knew as Mary about the four others.

'Two still in the Cells like yourself and two out Bay 1, but all of you coming along just fine.' Mary Hogg, knowing from the night of 30th December of Dame Ruth Dean's condition, and by the next afternoon that she was Jason's godmother and that he had not yet been told she had been on the train or was next door, hadn't named her. 'Did you take a look at any sitting around you?'

'I don't think – I just flaked out – no – yes – there was a girl with dark eyes and fair hair sitting opposite – dark eyes –'

'Och, that'll be wee Francesca Turner. She's doing just fine out Bay 1. Didn't need IT.' She saw his eyes smile. 'Nor'll you much longer, Jase, now you're up to remembering but one look at the bird was enough to get you fantasising. Get into the job, laddie – and just be leaving that wee electrode alone or you'll get the back of my hand.'

He grinned weakly. 'Mary, you're all TLC.'

'It's my tender loving care that pulls all the lads – just leave that to me and no more blethering just now.'

Good nurse, Mary. He hadn't wanted to talk more then. He had just wanted to lie and absorb the thought that the girl with those glorious eyes had come out alive. Mary had been a godsend in the Cells and he had quite liked Sandra Gilroy, Mary's usual partner, but hadn't cared much for the other IT staff nurses. They knew their jobs all right, but constantly gave him the impression that the patient was the one part of their job they found a drag.

He didn't want to think about them or the Cells now. He wanted to be sure she was still there.

Very carefully he turned his head to the right. He was in Bed 2. But the curtain on the left of Bed 3 was three-quarters drawn and all he could see was the lower third of her bed and plastered left leg up in a traction-splint. He turned his head back and sought contentment in the shadowy outlines on the greenish ceiling of Francesca Turner's head and pillows and resisted the urge to curse Staff Nurse Mastin, as he possessed that most rare of human qualities, gratitude. But for Staff Nurse Mastin, Francesca's bed would have been moved into mid-Bay 2 the day he was moved into Bay 1.

'I always speak my mind, Dr MacDonald, so I told our SNO, straight. Stimulating for patients you may call mixed wards, I said, but that's not what I call them. I call them not right, not decent, not kind. It may be much easier for the staff to have all the acutes and best equipment lumped together, I said, but if hospitals have started making life easier for the staff at the expense of the patients then it's no surprise to me, I said, they've had all these strikes. No strikes when I trained and I'll tell you for why. When I trained, we put the patients first – and don't try telling me – I said to the SNO – as any nurse or doctor as ever came out on strike does that seeing all of us that work in hospitals know first to suffer in any hospital strike has to be the patients. And patients, I said, suffer in mixed wards. Specially the women. And don't you try telling me otherwise, Dr MacDonald! I'm a woman and I know when a woman's ill she likes privacy and doesn't like being seen – specially when she's not so young – with tubes sticking out all over, her curlers in, teeth out, figure bulging or just plain honest old – and seeing you're a medic Dr MacDonald, I'll not mince it! She doesn't like being seen bouncing on and off a bedpan, or commode, or just pottering out to the toilet, by men – not even men in white coats. And don't you start on what about the male nurses, Dr MacDonald, or I'm like to tell you what I think on that! Just you tell me why in my training all the entrances to women's wards were screened off for bedpan rounds and every man in the hospital from the consultants down had to wait outside till the screens came down. Don't try telling me bedcurtains give enough privacy. When did you see the bedcurtain that was soundproofed, smellproofed? I'd not like to number the women I nursed in training that found that side hard enough to stomach amongst other women. Having to do it with men around – strange men – well! Like I said to our SNO, if you don't think that can be mental agony for many a woman, I do. And I don't like to think of putting that on top of any woman that's feeling right poorly and fretting cruel about hubby and the kiddies managing without her. Or when a woman's my old mum's age and never been seen in her nightie by any chap but her hubby and the family doctor. And I'm not saying, I said, it's not as bad for more than a few men. Not all men are Peeping Toms but there's more than a few that are as those that brought in the mixed wards should've reckoned. Plain to me as the nose on my face, I said, that those that brought it in knew as much about being hospital patients and bedside nursing as wouldn't fill a postage stamp. So I tell you this straight, I said to her, long as I'm permanent nights on Surgical A Bays, and seeing we admit less women than men as the women don't mostly ride the motorbikes, once out the Cells and whether likely to be knocked off or not, the women are having any corner beds going, with the wall the one side and the curtain drawn a good bit the other at night, or you'll have to find yourself another surgical night staff nurse!'

Jason's eyes slid sideways to Mr Halstead in Bed 1, that was nearest the entrance to the large alcove called the Nursing Bay. In the Holydale General, as in Martha's, the illest ward patients had the beds nearest the entrance. In the Holydale, 'likely to be knocked off'; in Martha's, 'likely to croak'; in plain English, 'likely to die'. In both hospitals it was customary for those ward patients making the most satisfactory progress to have the beds at the corners farthest from the entrance. For the last year in Surgical A, unless Staff Nurse Mastin was on holiday, women patients, whatever their progress, had the corner beds.

In common with most NHS hospitals, the Holydale General was desperately short of trained nurses. Staff Nurse Mastin was a very efficient surgical staff nurse, if, in the Senior Nursing Officer's private opinion, one of her most tedious old diehards whom circumstances forced her to accept on her staff. The SNO was only thankful that their ignorance of modern medical technology prevented their blocking the promotion of their juniors in age and, it had to be admitted, experience, but who had received the higher academic education that was so essential to the future of the nursing process. The youngish, highly qualified Senior Nursing Officer of the Holydale General invariably referred to her profession as 'the nursing process' and whilst not fully cognizant of the precise methods of operating the very latest medical machines, she had unbounded confidence in those possessed of this knowledge.

'My, my, Doc! We are an early bird,' softly cooed Nurse Douglas Smith, the third-year student night nurse. 'All ready for our little puff-up?'

'Hi, Doug. Time for BPs?' Jason reached for his watch on the bedside table set lengthways against the left side of his bed. The nightlights and the darkness of the northern English early morning sky outside the windows in the opposite wall had misled him into thinking he had woken in the small hours. 'So it is.'

'Early teas be in before we know it, dear.' Nurse Douglas Smith gently pushed up the pyjama sleeve and wound on the rubber bandage. He was a short, slender, fair, twenty-year-old, and much appreciated by his patients for the gentleness of his hands and nature. He wore a white coat, white shirt, blue bow tie to match his eyes, and the black cotton slacks he had bought in Holydale market and that drip-dried a treat. 'All done.' He deflated the bandage, unhitched his stethoscope. 'No use asking the reading, but who needs to ask? Know we're doing lovely now we're off all the blood and the drips – naughty me! Wash my mouth out with soap and water! Good thing Staff Mastin's along Bay 2. Intravenous infusions or IVIs at the pinch it's got to be, but let her hear "drip" – well, got four-letters hasn't it? I tell you no lie, Doc, if that woman heard, she'd do me!'

Jason grinned. 'Watch it, Doug. Dave Oliver says old Mastin's an ex-heavyweight and since he took over his TV and radio shop not one break-in though the last owner had to get in the glaziers every Sunday morning.'

'That Dave Oliver and his stories.' Doug waved delicately towards the eight-bedded ward across the Nursing Bay from the three-bedded Bay 1. 'Say anything to make a good story these reporters.'

'Not a reporter. Freelance journalist.'

'Gets his pieces in the papers. You know what they say – never believe what you read in the papers. No holding him now he's got his crutches. Shouldn't wonder if he puts us all in his pieces – the questions he asks – you'd not credit. But didn't we have a nice night for all we didn't want our tablets. Naughty, naughty! Staff Mastin's right – shocking patients, medics.'

'Sorry about that, but I loathe bloody knockouts. Few things irritate me more than feeling stoned out of my mind when I haven't enjoyed the stoning.'

'Never mind, dear. Just let's get comfy and we can have another nice little nap. Hang on to our strap – dig in our good heel – that's lovely. There. Now just let's check the pingies and toe-toes.' Very gently he raised in turn the limp white fingers and thumb of Jason's right hand, and without a change of expression Doug observed the increased tension in the long-jawed face that in these last nine days had so tightened and matured that the strength was far more apparent than the regularity of the bone structure. In the greenish lighting the fading bruises were yellow smudges, the healing cuts and grazes, charcoal smears, the overnight beard was black as the damp, untidy hair. Fretting him shocking, now he's up to what's what, thought Doug, and who'd wonder? Knows too much for his own good. Like that Dave Oliver said in the night, ONE-ARMED SURGEON OPERATES SINGLE-HANDED might rate banner headlines but he'd not fancy his chances of seeing it nor having his name on the byline if he did. Doug had told him he wasn't the only one.

He cooed, 'Doing lovely.'

'Care to bet?'

Doug smiled angelically. 'Not me, dear. Never seen the sense. Wouldn't be a bookie in the business if there was, would there? All comfy? Be good.'

Bright lad, thought Jason, mechanically picking up the cue as expected, 'Chance would be a fine thing.'

'Naughty, naughty!' Doug tripped lightly on to Mr Halstead.

Mr Halstead pretended to sleep through his blood-pressure check as he wasn't feeling up to a chat. He'd nothing against the boy. Obliging, kindly, youngster whose persuasions were his own business, if scarcely his responsibility, though poor Peggy wouldn't have seen it that way. Would have upset her badly, and if, in addition, she had found herself in a mixed ward, frankly Mr Halstead hadn't the present strength to dwell on what would have been her distress. It was a mercy she had been spared all this. 'And much else, Mr Halstead,' had said Benson very kindly when he broke the news on Mr Halstead's third day in the Cells. 'Your wife won't have known anything. Killed outright.'

'You – er – saw her, Mr Benson?'

'No, Mr Halstead. But Dr Patel, the senior house officer here, was one of those that helped lift out her body. I'm sorry to have to tell you this, sir, oh my word I'm sorry,' was all he had said about Peggy. Mr Halstead had not asked for more. Forty years ago he had not asked for more when a strange WREN had rung his mess to explain why Jean Gordon would be unable to keep her date with him that evening. He had then seen battle casualties; later he had seen thousands more; later still he had seen the worst that man could do to man when his Unit had been amongst the first Allies to reach Belsen. Thirty-six years after his first sight of that German concentration camp Mr Halstead's face twisted with a pain that had no connection with his fractured pelvis, the below mid-calf stump that ended his right leg, or his 'phantom' right foot. He had consciously to remind himself there was no wisdom in reflecting on evil, but much in recalling with great gratitude for poor Peggy that her death had come swiftly.

To the best of his recollection – and accurately – Benson had told him he had lost a foot as soon as he came properly round. 'Dr Patel had to amputate at the site. The foot was too damaged to repair and there was no other way of getting you out. Had he delayed, you wouldn't be here now. He did a neat job. I've only had to tidy the flap. We'll deal with your tin foot later. I'm telling you this now to save you the shock of discovering it for yourself. Do you follow what I'm saying, Mr Halstead?'

'Yes, doctor, but – er –'

'You're feeling pain from your right foot? You will. Briefly, the nerves need a parcel of time to inform the brain when a limb's missing. Till they do, you'll feel it. We call it the "phantom" limb. Do you follow me, Mr Halstead? Don't bother to say so. Just lift that right hand if you do . . . good . . . just take it easy. She'll do right . . .'

It had been after Benson had told him about Peggy that Mr Halstead asked about the other survivors and then, particularly about the two youngsters sitting with them. 'As I recall, brothers named Nigel and Simon.'

'Nigel and Simon Lenzie and doing right in Alanbridge General. Home in a few weeks.'

'Good. The others?'

Only one of their names had conveyed anything to him and on Peggy's behalf as much as his own, he asked, 'How is Dame Ruth Dean doing?'

'Coming along, Mr Halstead, coming along. Friend of yours?'

'Never met the lady, but my wife recognised her, having heard her speak.'

Mr Benson had let this go with a nod and made a mental note to pass this on to Lady MacDonald. Once the poor old bloke was up to visitors he'd need a parcel of help and though his sister-in-law Mrs Goodwin was a decent old body, she was no rest for tired eyes.

A day or so after that conversation the pretty redhead staff nurse had enquired in her soft, attractive if sometimes unintelligible to Mr Halstead, Scottish voice, if he minded the two young folk sitting away opposite. 'If wee Fran has it right. Soon as I described you to her, she'd you placed. A wee blonde with great dark eyes – you mind her, Mr H.? You do? Great! Aye, she's doing just fine and so's Jase – he's the big guy that faced her – and can you beat this? She's a nurse and he a medic and they'd to wait to find that out in Bay 1 – one of the wards out there. Francesca Turner's her name and she's just finished her third year up the Murrayfield General, Edinburgh – wait for it! He's Jason MacDonald and his dad was a big noise up the Murrayfield till he retired. Professor Sir George MacDonald, no less – real class we've in here just now,

Mr H.! Yourself, the Dame next door Mr Benson was saying you were asking for, Sir George and his lady wife in and out all day – 50p to talk to me the company I'm keeping – ach no! Jase MacDonald works down south. Surgical registrar at St Martha's, London – now flat on his bum out Bay 1 – can you beat that?'

'Most interesting. I'm glad all my fellow-survivors are doing so well.'

Mary Hogg's smiling green eyes held in their depth a disturbingly mature compassion for her age, twenty-three. The poor old guy had enough on his plate and from the look in his sunken grey eyes now he was coming out the drugs, a good canny mind. 'All just fine,' she insisted, untruthfully where Dame Ruth was concerned. 'You'll be meeting Fran and Jase when we shove you out Bay 1 in the morn. We lost Jase today. I'll be lost without you, Mr H. Aye the way of it in here. Working these Cells is like working on a factory belt – will you just watch yourself, hen! Leave that to me! Those wee drips are not due out just yet – ach, so you can smile? Keep that up and I'll be claiming a productivity bonus!'

'You deserve one, Staff Nurse Hogg.'

'You're just saying that, Mr H. But say it again!'

He missed Staff Nurse Hogg in Bay 1, but was otherwise relieved to be out of intensive therapy and free of all those tubes, electrodes and machines. So often in the Cells, when not attended by Staff Nurses Hogg and Gilroy, he had felt himself to be an additional item of machinery. The other intensive therapy staff nurses had, in the main, been pleasant girls, and if some had struck him as less considerate than others, human nature being what it was, that was only to be expected. He had found this particularly noticeable during those periods when for reasons that he lacked the medical knowledge to explain, he had been able to follow to a limited extent what was going on around him without being able to communicate this fact. He had a very clear recollection of hearing in one such period one staff nurse confiding to her colleague, 'I can't think why we have to waste our time saving this geriatric trash.'

Having a low opinion of human nature in general, in retrospect that diverted rather than offended him. It had not previously occurred to him to think of sixty-seven as 'geriatric' and he was sardonically amused by the medical attitude that apparently relegated sixty to being the official onset of senility whilst simultaneously accepting that for those in law and politics, the two professions that affected all lives more than any others, sixty could be regarded as comparatively young.

Poor Peggy – only sixty-one. Merciful indeed that she had been spared such a comment – and the problems that must ensue from his amputated foot. Useless to deny it was not a profound relief to know these would be his, alone. In their brief exchange on the subject yesterday, Benson seemed confident he'd have little trouble getting a good fit. 'I'm afraid we can't see to the tin foot up here. Have to be London.'

Mr Halstead regretted his new foot couldn't be fitted in the north of England, or preferably, Scotland. Margaret Goodwin was a sensible woman with whom he had always had a pleasant relationship; she had been remarkably and practically kind over this unhappy business. On the morning following the train crash she had closed her house, come down by hired car, booked in and, as were the MacDonald parents, was still staying at The Swan. She had visited him daily and dealt with all the inevitable legal formalities consequent on Peggy's death. 'I'll attend to it. Joe. You must rest, get back your strength, and take things quietly.' She had already admitted her concern over the prospect of his eventual return alone to the empty bungalow. 'Doesn't bear thinking on, Joe. Of course you must come to me for your convalescence. We'll discuss the matter later.'

He had been very touched, and silenced. How could he tell her – anyone – that the bungalow could never seem emptier than it had throughout these last seven years and how, each time he had returned from golf or garden, he had had to nerve himself to go back into his home. How could it ever be explained to any individual that thought loneliness the worst situation for anyone in health, how singularly fortunate must have been that first individual's life to have prompted that erroneous conclusion and concealed the truth that every human being is always alone.

A good, kind woman, Margaret Goodwin, and no small gestures from a widow in the mid-seventies, in midwinter, who was not even a blood-relative.

Peggy's married sister had rung from London from time to time and written to him expressing her condolences, sympathies and regrets at being prevented by domestic ties from attending the communal funeral service. Margaret had been driven to it by Sir George and Lady MacDonald with whom, understandably in the circumstances, she had struck up an empathetic friendship. The MacDonalds, either severally or together, now visited him daily. When his health allowed the time to be appropriate, he would ask the MacDonalds if they would care to come down to Peggy's memorial service in Wexhill. She would have liked a plaque in their church. He was vicar's warden. He would attend to that in due course. Margaret would certainly attend, and he would have to invite Peggy's sister and family. Probably her sister would come. He trusted so, for Peggy's sake, though he had never had much in common with her sister, a fact he had appreciated afresh every Christmas since his marriage.

Suddenly, belatedly, on that early morning in Bay 1 Mr Halstead realised he no longer need feel duty-bound to spend Christmas with his wife's only sister and family. The consequent flood of relief was so analgesic that it temporarily doused the sawing pain in his back, the heavy ache in his right leg, the prickling of his stump, the cramp in his 'phantom' and his own guilt at his relief. Death, he thought, in whatever circumstances was invariably a release for the living, if for the fortunate, a painful, unwanted, release. Having missed the fortune, he was spared the pain, for himself. Not Peggy. He grieved for her, but only for her. He gave a deep, relieved sigh and slid into a deep, restful, early morning sleep.

Jason was still awake and thinking about chance, Ruth Dean, and Dave Oliver's, 'Split down the middle, mate. Do I pack in the poker and stick to the typewriter? Or pack in the typewriter and stick to the decks?'

On Jason's penultimate day in the Cells, his mother, visiting him alone, had told him Ruth had been in the carriage. 'Still next door in 1, coming in here temporarily when you move out, then being moved to the one side-ward this hospital possesses. That's off Medical B, one floor up. They're turning it into a semi-IT cubicle. For obvious reasons we waited to tell you this.'

'Figures. Go on, Mum,' he muttered.

Gently, she told him the whole truth. Once he was in a Bay he would hear most of it from his fellow-patients and fill in the gaps for himself, and it would both help him and be preferable to handle the shock whilst still on his own. Being an only child he had the only child's habit, and in many cases including his, enjoyment of personal privacy. The news had distressed him more than he would have expected, not having realised how fond he had grown of old Ruth. 'She's part of our three lives,' his mother said, and he heard in her voice the echo of an old conversation begun long before his birth and for the first time in his life properly appreciated that his parents had had other and separate lives before their marriage and that Ruth Dean was the strongest thread connecting their pasts with their present.

'What's Dad say?'

'That the sooner she can be moved to Tom McNab's Gynae Unit in the Murrayfield, the better. Can't be done here. From her first night when Benson found it when he was taking a good look round to make sure there was no more damage, he'd intended transferring her to Alanbridge General soon as she was fit for it. He's quite content to shift her to the Murrayfield. Nearer than Martha's and she seems quite content to be done in the Murrayfield.'

'Christ. She's very low.' He reached with his left hand for his mother's. 'Sorry, Mum. All round.'

'I know, darling.' She had to pause. Then, 'She's low, but not that low. She knows the Murrayfield isn't her beloved Martha's, but she also knows the medical world and that any patient's best bet is to get into a good teaching hospital. The Murrayfield's one, Edinburgh's one, of the world's top medical centres, and in the Murrayfield, as she's told me, quote, "I'll have Mack breathing down the necessary necks." ' Her eyes smiled quickly, affectionately. 'Ruth right now is reminding Dad and me of Martha's itself in the war. Battered to pieces, piles of rubble everywhere, and strung up on sheets across the few still standing blocks in huge letters, ST MARTHA'S HOSPITAL. DOWN BUT NOT OUT.' She blinked quickly. 'Corny, yes, but true. Like Ruth now.'

She had not said more and he'd been grateful. She was a chatty soul, but she'd always recognised when he, or his father, didn't want to talk. Unlike Dave – but that was only because the poor guy had to talk. And relive it.

Dave Oliver had been the only person to show Jason the newspaper photographs of the derailed, divided train and the remains of the second carriage. In the earlier editions the photographs had been taken before the remains had been shrouded in tarpaulin; only the rear third bore visible traces that it had once been part of a railway carriage. Jason hadn't wanted to see those pictures. He had worked too long in an Accident Unit to need tangible evidence of the pictures in his mind. In the Cells his parents had given him only the kind of brief account of the crash that if left unspoken would have deafened all three. None of the nurses but Mary Hogg had mentioned it. Mary was blunt, 'A bloody awful stramash and could I but get my hands on the wee tearaways that set it up they'd be needing intensive therapy but not getting it from me – will you stop pulling at that strapping, hen!'

'Hell, Mary, it's so bloody itchy –'

'I'm awful sorry about that, but you'll have to sweat it out, hen. Just sweat it out . . .'

Francesca knew it had to be sweated out. Dave had to talk it out.

When Jason was moved into Bay 1, at first it was into Mr Halstead's present space. Bed 2 had then been occupied by one of the quartet of teenage motor-cyclists now all up-patients in assorted plasters in Bay 2. He had been moved in midmorning; Francesca's bedcurtains had been open; she had been propped in a sitting position, and over the youth recovering from an anaesthetic in Bed 2 had nodded unsmilingly at Jason and called quietly, 'Hallo, again.'

He had expected to see her in that bed and, from his mother's and Mary Hogg's descriptions, that her face would be as marked as his own. He hadn't expected to find the sight of her soft, dark, golden hair fallen over her scarred forehead, cheeks, cut lips, and badly bruised dark eyes so profoundly disturbing that he nearly forgot to return her greeting. He raised his left hand. 'Hi, there.' That was all they had then said to each other, and they were still exchanging the same guarded looks of two people aware they had just shared the same escape from death that neither could yet tolerate putting into words, when one of the day student nurses closed the curtains round Bed 2.

A very few minutes later a slight, grey-haired man in dressing gown and pyjamas with the right trouser leg slit down both seams and fixed with outsize safety-pins over the plaster on the outstretched right leg, had deftly propelled his wheel-chair to the left side of Jason's bed. Jason had guessed the man's identity but been puzzled, having heard the guy was thirty-one. At that time, the long, thin, sensitive, bruised face looked old enough for the grey hair and behind the smile the brown eyes were still in the nightmare.

'Hi, there! Me, Dave Oliver, you Jase MacDonald. Welcome back to the living, mate! I was sitting two up from you with your and my mate the lovely DBE in between.' Dave tapped one side of his scarred nose with a scarred forefinger. 'Your lovely Mum's given me the whole inside story . . .'

Christ, did the poor guy have to talk?

'. . . Meanwhile back at the ranch – old Halstead's in Cell 3 – er – your Mum did say you'd heard –? Right then, so's he now, poor old guy. He, you and I got it most down the right. The lovely Fran and the DBE caught it mostly left and we all caught it in the kisser. Saw you having a how-do with Fran when I got this job rolling down Bay 2 – where was I? With you! Right load of plug-uglies we must've looked when they scraped us out and wheeled us in – right tough on the women – or is that sexist? Anyhow – the Almighty Oz's told the lovely Fran few weeks time the scars should be fading nicely and your Mum says same for the DBE. Coming along nicely the DBE, your Mum says, and being shifted up to the side-ward off Medical B tomorrow. Dead classy side-ward, Mum says – only one in this joint – but the DBE rates the bit of quiet as she's still having the headaches. I reckon you rate the bit of class if you rate a DBE – had her a bit off in the – had her lined up in education not nursing – so who's perfect? Lovely lady the DBE. Sends me kindly message via Mum and your lovely Mum's my mate but good! Always comes over for a chat – not a word to the Sir – though he stops by for a how-do to me and Fran when coming in and out to you. Good to see you out of the Cells. How does it feel to be one of the ones that got away?' Suddenly the mask dropped off. 'Bloody peculiar, eh?'

'Bloody.'

'You do not joke, mate!' The mask was hauled back on. 'There was me – front seat on the story that hit every bloody front page – banners – the lot! And I had to read all about it! There they all were straight into the Brits being British – Dunkirk – the Blitz – straight into it. No panic, no screams, no hysteria, just got themselves out the uprights, formed themselves into rescue squads, swiped crowbars and ladders from guards' vans, lifted down old ladies and kiddiwinks. Villagers horsed out with blankets and cups of tea – couldn't spit without hitting good human interest copy! No looting, no pushing, no shoving – everybody out – after you, mate! And I had to bloody read all about it! Shouldn't happen to a Chinaman as my old Gran used to say before the booze got her at ninety-four. Knew how to handle it, did my old Gran. Married late, same as my Mum but she and dear old Dad had the shorter innings. Old Gran outlived the lot but me. Not sure why. Not sure about anything after this turn-up.' Again the mask fell off exposing the full horror. 'Why us, mate? Why – us?'

Jason looked straight into the haunted brown eyes. 'Not knowing, chum, can't say.'

Jason, listening to the regular rhythm of Mr Halstead's sleeping respirations, to the subdued chorus of sleepy voices just floating across from Bay 2, and longing for the early morning tea to make the inside of his mouth taste less foul, and for his morning wash and the remaking of his bed that in Surgical A Bays would be done by the day nurses after the patients' breakfasts, thought back to his words that had terminated his first conversation with Dave Oliver. The words ran round and round his mind whilst his gaze moved upwards to the ceiling over Bed 3, then sideways to his plastered right arm; upwards and sideways; upwards and sideways; as if he were a puppet with all the strings broken but those that moved his eyes and that those intact strings could only move in two directions.

5

The ghostly feathers of snow floating down from the dark, late afternoon January sky, began laying a pristine plaster on the outsides of the windows in the wall opposite the three well-spaced beds backed against the internal wall of Bay 1. Lined up against the window wall in their usual waiting places were the ward's resuscitation trolley and the one ventilator the hospital possessed. Twenty minutes ago the latter had been pushed back in place by an uncharacteristically silent Mary Hogg.

Being a Saturday afternoon, Jason had been put back to bed early, before tea, by one of the two physiotherapists on call for the weekend, and the two day student nurses on the 12.15 to 8.45 p.m. shift that day. Owing to his height, normal, and the additional weight of his plasters, helping him to balance on his good leg, in and out of a wheelchair and the high bed, was physically demanding on all concerned and the process still left him exhausted. Though he had refused to admit this, it was common knowledge to the staff and his fellow patients from one look at his pale, sweating face. Mr Halstead now habitually engrossed himself in a book immediately Jason was back in bed, and Dave Oliver perched himself on Francesca's locker-seat to keep her attention diverted until poor old Jase was up to the next round – but if ever a guy needed his head examined . . .

Jason listened absently to Dave's involved account of his last holiday in Greece and sensed Fran was only waiting for him to open his mouth to start another argument. God alone knew why he made her so aggressive. He didn't. He didn't want to fight with her. All he wanted – Christ, he didn't know what the hell he wanted where she was concerned. All he knew was that there was damn all he could do about her, or anything, whilst still anchored in these damned hot plasters with the question-mark still hanging over his right arm. If the answer to the arm was, no – rows of other question-marks. He longed to be able to talk to her – just talk – just explain that he understood the hell she was going through stuck in bed tied to that traction-splint and having to keep up the act that she didn't give a damn that neither her father nor new stepmother had bothered to visit her, and that all her father's telephone enquiries and gifts of expensive flowers had been dealt with by his secretary. The stepmother had written once '. . . love to come up but all this snow . . . so far north . . .' The distance and the weather hadn't stopped her old nanny from rushing up from Kent on the day after and according to Dave, spending two nights in a bed-and-breakfast in the high street. 'Dear old dad's had to fly to Brussels on business,' confided Dave in the comparative privacy of the up-patients' dayroom. 'No one's told me Newcastle's airport's closed. If he can't use the company jet, he'll have smaller jobs and choppers waiting for him to pick up a phone.'

'He's that loaded?'

Dave nodded: 'I've more than the odd mate on the city pages. Know his name.'

'Christ. No wonder she's so stroppy, poor girl.'

Dave glanced at him oddly, wondered if to open his big mouth, then looked at Jason's right arm and settled for another nod.

'. . . so there I was in Athens, cleaned-out, when this guy says . . .'

Jason looked at Mr Halstead reading a John le Carré, at the returned ventilator, at Benson talking to the sister sitting behind the eggshell-blue fibreglass nursing counter, at the falling snow. He saw Benson look at the windows and the silent anger in the cherubic profile and his own face tightened in empathy.

'This snow'll have that driver happy as a bastard on Father's Day, sister,' drawled Mr Benson, 'and that's how I bloody feel at having to pack the poor young bastard off to the living cemetery.'

Sister Preston, the larger, fairer and younger of the two day sisters that alternated in charge of Surgical A replied placidly, 'All our ambulance drivers are very experienced and used to the moor roads in all weathers, Mr Benson.'

'Too bloody right, sister.' Mr Benson swung round, shot across the Nursing Bay, down the left corridor and through the glass swing doors to the stairs and lifts as if Surgical A were on fire.

Sister Preston sighed with placid relief and kept her attention fixed on the rows of unlit bulbs and three blank monitor screens set into the top of her counter. Far wiser not to notice the obviously heated exchange going on between Dr Meredith and Mary Hogg in Cell 1, the only lighted of the three temporarily patientless cubicles. Staff Nurses Hogg and Gilroy were clearing and resetting into immediate readiness Cell 1, before going off-duty for the evening. Dr Meredith was the house officer on-call for the weekend. Sister Preston didn't know why Dr Meredith had returned to Surgical A and gone straight into 1 some minutes ago and she didn't wish to know. It would only mean unpleasantness. Sister Preston disliked unpleasantness and anyway, she had to watch over her counter.

The bulbs were connected to the easily accessible nurse-call and well-concealed emergency buttons that, as the piped oxygen, were fitted into every bed in Surgical A. When a nurse-call button was pressed, the respective bulb glowed a steady green. When an emergency, the bulb flashed on and off in red and simultaneously emitted a softly piercing rapid bleeping. The monitor screens were extensions of the bedside cardiac monitors in the intensive therapy cubicles.

All so nice and quiet. Bay 2, neat and empty, as with the exception of Mr Oliver, all the Bay 2s were in the dayroom watching television under the supervision of the two student nurses. Mr Oliver and Miss Turner were obviously enjoying their quiet chat, Dr MacDonald enjoying listening and dear old Mr Halstead his spy book. If only – oh, dear, still at it! But still, so nice and quiet now the nursing auxiliaries had cleared away the bed-patients' teas, and likely to remain so until 'visitors' at six.

Sister Preston took another peek at Bay 1. The SNO was so right. Mixed wards stimulated both sexes. Such a wise woman and so helpful to send a male staff nurse to help out in the Bays over this weekend as both were full and as she said, no one could be sure when the Cells would fill again. Of course, if they had a sudden inrush, the four from the train could be moved straight up to Surgical B instead of waiting till Tuesday. 'We've got the bloody beds, sister,' said Mr Benson, 'and whilst we have those four'll stay where they are till over their fourteenth night. Save me a parcel of insomnia knowing they're in quick reach of the equipment down here if any of them spring anything. No sign of that yet. Seldom is till it bloody happens. And I like my sleep, oh my word I do.'

Such a nice man, Mr Benson, when you got used to him and his habit of always looking on the black side. And, naturally, a bit upset about that poor young man this afternoon. Just one of those things, unfortunately. He had quite upset Sister Preston. She could do with her tea when the male staff nurse returned from his to relieve her. She hadn't worked with him before, but he seemed very nice. She liked working with male nurses and couldn't understand why her colleague, Sister Yates, objected to them and 'their habit of always nicking the top jobs'. Sister Preston had to tell Sister Yates that she, personally, found the men so much more dependable as they didn't have babies. Oh dear – still at it!

The Cells were invisible from the heads of the beds in Bay 1 but Dave Oliver noticed Mr Benson streaking from the counter. He broke off in mid-sentence, mentally switched on his mental tape-recorder, and demanded, 'What's into the Almighty Oz, Jase?'

'Doesn't fancy defeat.'

'Where's the defeat? He had to transfer the guy. Alanbridge has the neurosurgical unit.'

'Corrections, Dave,' put in Francesca in her most detached tone. 'Two. Alanbridge has a neurosurgical ward. Not a proper unit. No neurosurgical theatre. And the Oz hasn't just transferred a guy. A human vegetable.

'You reckon?' Dave looked at Jason, who stayed silent.

'From what Doug said last night, even if Alanbridge had an N.S. theatre, the skull and brain were too grossly damaged to benefit from neurosurgery. Can't expect much else if you don't bother to do up your safety-belt, then crash your car at high speed into a phone box and shoot head first through windscreen and box.' Above the lace pie-crust frilled collar of her pink silk and lace bedjacket, Francesca's lovely eyes and healing face mirrored the detachment in her voice and suddenly reminded Jason of his mother telling him that in one of her telephone conversations with the SNO of the Murrayfield General about Francesca's progress in the Holydale, that SNO had described her as so highly gifted academically that she would undoubtedly have done well in medicine. The girl has the right detachment, she said.

'So what happens to him in Alanbridge?'

'He'll be in that ward for the foreseeable future. Only he won't see it. Vision may be unaffected but brain's switched off. I know what that means. Last autumn I had three months in the Murrayfield's Neurosurgical B. We've got a proper unit, and first-rate neurosurgeons. The Bs they can't help – and that ward's the nearest thing to hell anyone can see on this earth.'

Jason stared into the midair and his healing face took on an inherited rigidity it had only worn in the Holydale General. Only Mr Halstead, glancing sideways, saw the left hand dangling over the side of Jason's bed suddenly tighten to a fist. Mr Halstead opened his mouth to say something, then closed it without saying anything.

Dave persisted, 'What's really bugging the Oz? Head or heart?'

Francesca looked at Jason with the open irritation his apparent ability to withdraw into a private place invariably aroused in her. Typical. Bloody typical. She chose her words as a weapon but, being irritated, chose rashly. 'I'll bet he's spent the last thirty-six hours stalling the vultures.' Before the words were out she sensed Dave stiffening like a terrier at a rat-hole. She added hastily, 'Could be wrong.'

Dave ignored the rider. 'Hungry for a strong young heart, kidneys and that lot? That right, Jase?'

'Don't ask me. Never have time to read the Sunday papers.'

'Come off it, mate! We all know it happens.'

Jason looked at him. 'You may. I don't.'

'Hell, Jase – why not? No use to him. Could save others.'

'Still his property, Dave.'

'As of now. But there must be times when the machines get switched off – earlyish. Right?'

'Never seen that or heard of it in Martha's. I'm not

saying we haven't our quota of surgeons that I wouldn't allow to take a splinter out of my little finger, but I've never come across or heard of one with homicidal tendencies.'

Francesca knew she should keep her mouth shut, but her irritation had been increased to anger by Dave's insistence on Jason's confirmation. And again, bloody typical! I'm just a woman - only a nurse - only had three years' experience - what the hell do I know that's worth knowing? I'm a Registered General Nurse - that's the Scottish equivalent of the SRN - I've got a Diploma of Life Sciences and Nursing - and both treat me as if I've just started as a nursing auxiliary -

'Is it really murder?' She dropped the words like stones.

Jason's face jerked towards her and his expression, but not his brain, softened. You can look so lovely - and if you'd only let yourself I'm sure you could be so lovely - and God knows you're not stupid, but - Christ! 'Ask Dave,' he said drily. 'Words are his trade. Ask him to come up with another for a premeditated killing.'

She flushed with fury that he mistook for painful embarrassment. He wanted to hit himself and grimaced as if he had.

Dave's keen eyes watching both were half-amused, half-sad. He switched off the mental recorder. 'Like I was saying - meanwhile back at the Athens ranch . . .'

Mr Halstead lowered his book to think his own thoughts. This period in close proximity to these three youngsters had been interesting and salutary, particularly as regards Francesca. In many ways, physically, she continued to remind him of his memory of Jean Gordon, but in other ways, of Peggy. Something in the tone of the girl's voice, in her manner, in her determination to press a subject in the hope of provoking an unnecessary scene, in her impatience when that provocation failed, in her aura of 'Why should I sympathise with you when I am suffering so much?' - kept recalling to him, Peggy.

Would Jean have proved the same, had she lived, had they married? It had long been his comfort that he had known her too well to fear that; but too well, in those wartime weeks, hadn't covered cohabitation. They had never slept together or spent one night under the same roof. All he had been able to do was kiss and hold her in the short precious intervals that were all the war, and their conventions, allowed. Inevitably, in those meetings – as always for the young in love – they had been on their best behaviour and showed only those sides they thought the other wished to see. Impossible to maintain that situation in marriage, or when neighbours in hospital beds. Would Jean Gordon have proved to have come from the same mould?

It hurt him to think she could ever have proved other than the sweet, warm loving girl in long memory. But he had seen too much and liked too little of what he'd seen to delude himself that he was exempt from common human failings. He had too often observed how people, throughout their lives, continued to be physically attracted to one particular type of the opposite sex.

Turning this over in his mind, evoked a much older memory. The memory of a friend of his young manhood who had borne certain similarities to young Dave, saying, 'If you marry, Joe, watch your step. You've no sister. Your mother's a kind woman devoted to your father and yourself, so the chances are you'll fall for bitches. I won't. Lay your last bob on that. My mamma and sisters are pure bitch. I know what to avoid. You don't.'

No. He hadn't. Nor, he surmised, would young Jason, though he was an astute, stoic and kindly chap whom Mr Halstead would have been happy to allow a very useful overdraft. Dave? Mr Halstead's firm mouth twitched upwards at the corners. Good company, good guts – but £10 at the outside. Francesca? Only with her father's written assurance that he was prepared to be her corollary. The omniscient Dave had given him the poor child's background and whilst he had every sympathy with her in this respect, he doubted that she had any clearer idea of the real value of money than she appeared to have of the real value of humanity. Neither were her responsibility; inhumanity begat inhumanity as violence, violence. She was far from the first child of a man of substance whom Mr Halstead had encountered, that had been over-indulged financially and the reverse, emotionally.

Up to the night of 30th December last, he would have considered it strange that such a girl should have chosen to enter the nursing profession. His only previous experience of hospital life had been two weeks in a military hospital in Egypt in '43 after being rushed in with acute appendicitis. All the other chaps in the huge ward had been wounded in the desert and were mostly in massive plasters. It had been a junior officers' ward, captains and under, with twenty beds each side, and never whilst he was there with more than two young QA sisters and two RAMC orderlies on duty during the day; at night, one young QA and one orderly. All day, all night, neither sisters nor orderlies had stopped running up and down that ward. All three sisters had complained volubly about their feet, the heat, the Army, the MOs, the lack of equipment, but never in his hearing of their hard, back-breaking work or their patients. Once he had asked the Irish QA what she was doing in the British Army. 'Honest to God, Captain Halstead, if it's the truth you're after – I was clean round the ruddy bend when I signed up.'

Very different situation here. Infinitely quieter and so luxuriously appointed that he might well be in an expensive private hospital. Interesting to observe that some of the millions collected in taxation had been put to good use and also, he thought with dry amusement, how, no doubt purely by chance, many of his fellow patients in both Bays bore testimony of the ability of the middle classes to avail themselves of the available benefits to which they had made full financial contribution. Young Dave had noted this last: 'From where I sit and swing around this joint, Mr H., your average NHS patient has gone upmarket. You reckon that was what old Nye Bevan had in mind?'

Excellently appointed; reasonable meals; and in the Bays, reasonable service, if in the main, impersonal as a dentist's waiting room. A similarity enhanced by attitudes and appearances of the nursing staff in their skimpy white, blue or grey apronless uniform dresses. Remarkably similar to dentists' receptionists that, when necessary, turned dental nurses. In fairness, some of the Bay nurses were very efficient, but with the delightful exceptions of Staff Nurses Mastin, Hogg, Gilroy and young Doug, the attentions of the other nurses afforded him no more pleasure than he appeared to afford them. 'All right are you?' those others asked on leaving him and left without waiting for the answer.

If this insight was typical of the new order, he thought Francesca had probably chosen the right career. He had no doubt she was very efficient, and would enjoy the impersonality and the authority. All she lacked was the warmth exuded by those three QAs long ago, those three staff nurses and Doug, here. That was the missing piece. Warmth. Not the child's fault, but missing from her as from poor Peggy. And Jean? In view of the law of averages – regrettably, only too probably.

Mr Halstead sighed a small sigh for the sudden death of a long-cherished illusion and then a small ironic smile lit his less sunken grey eyes. The advancing years had many advantages, but to his mind, the greatest of these was the advantage of experience. He glanced at Jason, and as his stump was hurting, sought comfort from his book.

'Hold it, folks!' Dave's sharp ears had caught the opening of a cell door and the upraised voices. He heaved himself on to his crutches, swung to the foot of Mr Halstead's bed from where he could see all round the Nursing Bay and Dr Meredith and Mary Hogg glaring at each other's red faces just outside Cell 1. 'Stay tuned for a ball-by-ball,' he muttered happily.

Sister Preston behind the counter was deaf, dumb, but not blind. She had to watch the lifeless bulbs and monitors.

'Don't – don't you dare talk to me like that, Staff!'

'And what's so special about you, hen?'

Dr Meredith was the same age, half a head shorter and two stones heavier than Mary Hogg. Dr Meredith had been educated in an English girls' public school – sixth form boys admitted after suitable vetting; a plate-glass university renowned for its advanced views and the high unemployment rate of its graduates; and St Benedict's Hospital, London. After qualifying, she had worked her pre-registration in Benedict's amongst nurses from domestic backgrounds largely akin to her own. She'd never had any problems, nor actually much to do with the Benedict's nurses – of course they'd been uneducated cows – nurses always were – but this little scrubber from the Gorbals or wherever was a typical Glaswegian and precisely why

Dr Meredith had refused to contemplate working in Scotland or so much as crossing the Border. 'Will you stop calling me "hen"! My title is "Doctor"!'

Francesca closed her eyes instinctively. Fool! Walked in!

Jason stared at his bedtable. Duck, woman – duck!

Mary's reply echoed round both Bays. 'Is that a fact? Why's no one told me you're a Member of the Royal College of Physicians? Or is it the M.D. or just a Ph.D. you've up your sleeve? And if not, hen – why's no one told you "Doctor"s' but a courtesy title to which crummy house officers with but the M.B., B.S. are not – in fact – entitled? Did you not know? Ach, I'll give you more – I'm big-hearted. Has no one told you right now one in ten with your crummy qualifications are out the dole queue? But if you've heard of one young SRN with IT training on social security – you tell me! And if you think you can do the job for me and my pals – feel free! Make the right balls-up with the bloody wee machines you'd have made this morning had we not sorted it for you in time. But don't be thinking we did it to save your wee neck! We did it for the poor wee man we've just had to shove on. He was our patient. We're here for our patients and not to wait on the likes of you. We're not handmaidens to the bloody Gods – and don't you forget it! We're nurrrses! Just you try the once more shoving me your dirty trolley to clear away and you'll get it back in your teeth! You'll do your own dirty work and I'll do mine! But you've wasted enough of my time – I've a job to do if you've not!' Mary shot back into the cubicle, closed the glass door quietly behind her then released further energy by pulling from the dress pocket under her gown the airway, tracheal dilators, and artery forceps for moving aside tongues, without which she never appeared on-duty, and flinging them on the bed Staff Nurse Gilroy was remaking. 'Bloody women medics!'

'Cool it, Mary. Saturday evening and we're off in ten minutes.'

'Now don't you start, Sandra! My adrenalin's that up I'm like to do you and finish the reset in five!'

Dr Meredith, after a furious backward glance at Sister Preston in rapt contemplation of her counter and the grinning Dave, walked with as much dignity as she could muster out of the Nursing Bay and through the glass swing doors. 'God, nurses! Pointless reporting this to that Antipodean chauvinist. He'd back the bitch! He always backed the ITs and she knew why! Just bloody typical of the anti-feminism of the whole male-orientated British medical profession that he kept underlining with his insistence on tying her weekends on with his own! God, this dump that dared call itself a hospital and had only Surgical A not overdue for the knacker's yard! God, why did Surgical A have to have that red-haired bitch of a refugee from Page 3! God – oh God – why wouldn't they do up their seat belts? The car's bonnet had buckled into the phone box but the driver's seat, wheel and steering column had survived intact. What in hell was the use of doing medicine when so many times there was bugger-all good you or anyone could do and you just had to stand there trying not to scream at your own uselessness!'

Dave swung back to Francesca's locker seat. 'If there's one thing I like about the quiet ordinary life in a quiet ordinary hospital ward on a quiet ordinary Saturday afternoon, it's watching the lovely Mary doing a GBH on poor little Fatso.'

Francesca's intelligence forced her to admit, 'Meredith had it coming.'

Jason felt very weary, very old and as if he had been born with that heavy ache in his arm and his mind. He knew this had torn two ways Francesca's strong feminist views and for her sake wished to God that Meredith had been a guy, even although his common sense forced him to accept that in that event, almost certainly, the scene wouldn't have occurred. He didn't have to fancy Mary to recognise she was too pretty, sexy and good at her job for any male medic in his right mind to chance getting into the big doctor act when she was around. He said to no one in particular, 'Being beaten-up by nurses is an occupational hazard for all H.O.s and registrars.'

Mr Halstead sensed the new tension in the atmosphere had been caused by Staff Nurse Hogg's not unamusing outburst, without fully comprehending why this should be. He heard the exhaustion in Jason's tone and put his book on his chest. 'You seem to speak with the voice of experience, Jason.'

'Scars to prove it, Mr H.'

'Why did they tell me wrong?' wailed Dave. 'Why did they kid me all nurses love doctors?'

'Some do. Some marry 'em.' Francesca's contempt was open. 'They're good financial propositions. Big money in medicine these days – even you junior hospital medics are scarcely on the breadline.' She glanced at Jason staring fixedly into mid-air. 'You lot never stop griping about working 120 or whatsit hours per week – you leave out the bit that for quite a few of those hours you're not actually working but hanging about on-call. And you don't over-stress what your UMTIES come to – those are their Units of Medical Time, Dave, and they add up rather healthily – as do perks like ash cash – cremation fees. Very paying proposition modern medicine.' She smiled coldly. 'Which could explain why so many medics' offsprings read medicine. Suffering humanity nicely rewards with status and cash those medically qualified to help its sufferings – and there's nothing new about those helpers being unaverse to helping themselves, if there's any truth in the apocryphal story of your cherished Nye Bevan saying he only managed to put over the NHS by putting gold into the consultants' pockets. It was a little unfortunate that Nye Bevan – as some others in high places since – apparently either forgot or was ignorant of the fact that most of the work in any hospital is, and always has been, done by the nurses.'

There was a deafening, static silence. She refused to let it disturb her. She knew they had taken her attack as directed personally at Jason, and his parents to whom they thought she should be grateful. Why? She hadn't asked the MacDonalds to keep visiting her, or ringing the Murrayfield on her behalf. She was bored out of her mind with people thinking she ought to be grateful. For what? She hadn't asked to be born – smashed up on that bloody train – or for all of those godawful flowers. She'd never asked for anything, but all her life . . . thank Daddy, love, and aren't you a lucky little girl! Thank your Dad, Francesca, and aren't you a lucky girl! Thank your father, dear, and aren't you a lucky young lady! Thank – thank – yuck!

Mr Halstead ended the silence by flicking his book onto the floor and sighing loudly in his vain efforts to retrieve it.

'Hold it, Mr H.!' Dave heaved himself up and swung

over and Sister Preston reseated herself on her high stool. She saw Staff Nurse Hogg before Dave, carefully lowering himself for the book, felt two strong young arms hooking themselves under his armpits from behind and levering him upwards. 'Hey, thanks, but – oh, thanks, Mary!'

'So I should think, hen.' Mary Hogg, slender and shapely in her unstarched, short-sleeved, zip-fronted white uniform dress with an open turned-down collar and the rim of her paper cap a white halo on her short, slightly curling, freshly combed red-gold hair, propped her knuckles on her hips. 'If you've to bust that plaster you'll oblige me by waiting till I'm off-duty.' She picked up the book. 'Let's give those pillows a wee turn, Mr H. From the look, not before time.' She slid one hand gently under the back of his head. 'Careful now. Mind that wee pelvis. Okay, Mr H.?'

'Most comfortable, thank you. Finished for the day?'

'And my thirty-seven-and-a-half-hour week. See you Tuesday – no, I'll not. My half-day. I'll not be on till one when you lot'll have been moved up Surgical B.'

'So Mr Benson was saying this morning. Surgical semi-convalescent, I gather.'

'That's a fact. Top floor and grand views. You, Fran and Jase'll maybe be up there a few weeks. As for you, hen –' she tipped her head at Dave,' they'll be chucking you away out in no time.'

His thin, less pale; haunted and once more young face smiled into hers. 'Mary, my love, my sweet,my own – don't say such things! They can't turn me out to hop alone into the cold, cold, snow.'

'You'll do just fine in a new walking plaster and on elbow crutches after the physios have sorted you.'

Dave shuddered dramatically and had his mental tape recorder back on. He had noticed the hot war had been turned to cold when Mary mentioned Tuesday. He didn't look at Jason or Francesca as he asked innocently, 'Why not shift us Monday? Clean start to the week.'

Mary saw that Francesca looked about to specify the potential dangers to post-severe traumatic injuries and post-operative patients in certain categories on the tenth to fourteenth day after the event, and got in first. 'Our Mr Benson has this wee freak about having his patients in beds. Suggest they'll do just fine on mattresses on the floor – he'll blow his mind. There's no sweat for these beds here just now, but only the floor for you up Surgical B till Tuesday, so here you stay. But I can't keep my boyfriend hanging about the front hall whilst I'm blethering here. I'll be up Surgical B to see you lot. And mind you take care of yourself whilst I'm away, Mr H.'

'Thank you very much for that and so much else, Staff.'

'Mr H. how many times? The name's Mary.'

He smiled up at her. 'As the song says, "Sweet as any name could be." QED.'

'Getaway!' She blushed and rounded on the young men. 'Why can't you two come up with that like? If you want to start pulling the birds just you have a wee chat with our Mr H. Isn't that a fact, Fran?'

Francesca smiled with her lips. 'Spot on, Mary.'

Mary glanced at Jason. She had noticed his face before steadying Dave. She looked deliberately at his right arm, caught his eye and winked. 'Not dropping off. Ach, well. There's my hard-earned pay-packet down the drain.'

Having been qualified six years, Jason could read a patient's prognosis in the lift of a colleague's eyebrow across a bed. Being in a bed it took a couple of seconds before his eyes looked as if someone in his brain had pressed a button that brilliantly illuminated twin, dark blue bulbs. He liked and trusted Mary – and so, he knew, did Benson. He said, a little unsteadily, 'Take Doug's tip and don't bet. Can't see the sense, he says.'

'The wee man's right. Got a good canny head whatever he's not got. He's okay, is Doug, though mind you, if I'd a vase, I'd put him in it.' She sailed off, swaying her hips, to Dave's shout of laughter. She had reached the middle of the Nursing Bay when Jason had to turn to share his joyous relief with Francesca and saw her suddenly slump back against her pillows.

Jason's low, urgent, 'Mary!' was immediately echoed by the soft, piercing bleeping of the solitary bulb flashing on and off in red on the blue counter. His finger was still on the concealed emergency button in his bedhead that his left hand had found instinctively when he turned to Francesca, when Mary, a white streak of movement, with one hand swept the resuscitation trolley to Francesca's bedside and with the other switched on Bed 3's piped oxygen supply. Already Sister Preston's thumb was pressed down on the large red button on her counter that instantly alerted to the ward the hospital's Cardiac Arrest team. Day or night, weekdays or weekends, a team was on permanent call. The individual members varied, not the team itself.

In well under five minutes the little posse of white coats and white uniform dresses had disappeared behind the curtains closed round Bed 3. For those, and the next fifteen minutes, Mr Halstead, and Dave on his locker-seat, in silence avoided each other's eyes and kept glancing at the whitened knuckles of Jason's left hand gripping his top bedhead rail and at the sweat pouring down Jason's white, rigid, helpless, hopeless face.

Twenty-five minutes after that low, urgent 'Mary!', Mary Hogg, white-lipped and expressionless, quietly closed Jason's right and front curtains, then Mr Halstead's left and front, leaving the three men in an enclosed, twin-bedded cubicle. She looked only once at Jason's face and when she did the truth was in her sad green eyes. Jason didn't see her. He didn't see the two men with him, or hear, as they heard, the soft rumble of the especially deep stretcher-trolley with the special red blanket and special white pillow. He knew what was going on and that this must happen. He had known from his last look at Francesca Turner's closed face that she had already left the train.

6

'Was it worth it?'

Dave blinked, 'Come again, mate?'

The taximan dumped the holdall beside the elbow crutches propped against the back seat. He was about Dave's age but larger and darker and his voice fell like soft water from his lips. 'Was the skiing worth coming back with that plaster?'

'Oh, sure.' He could see the mountains, the pristine snow, the pistes, the slowly moving multicoloured frieze of the skiers hooked to the cable-lift, the swaying dots of the chairlifts and the black wedge of the cablecar high over the snow-buried firs in the ravine. 'Wouldn't have missed it.'

'That a fact? Where'd you go?'

'Heilig Tal.'

'Where's that?'

'Austrian Tyrol. Small joint.'

'That'll be why it's new to me.' The driver shut the door, climbed into his seat, and called back through the half-open glass partition, 'Cost a packet?'

'Dead cheap.'

'Och, aye? I'll have to be remembering it. I go up Aviemore. Was there last month. Good snow. If you've not tried the Cairngorms you should when that's back in the one piece.'

'You're on,' Dave vowed with total, if transitory, sincerity. The only winter sports he'd seen had been on colour television. At school and university he couldn't afford it. On his various papers he had taken all his holidays in summer and on one first met his ex-wife. Bloody Benidorm. Since turning freelance, when he'd had the time, he'd never had the money, or vice versa, and at any time the money had been subsidised by cards. He hadn't touched a deck, since . . .

The taxi drew away from the glass-roofed frontage of Waverley Station and crawled in the one-way line of cars and taxis moving up the short, steepish exit that opened into the wide Waverley Bridge Road. At the top the driver had to wait for a gap in the on-coming traffic before turning right towards Princes Street. And straight ahead, poised over Old and New City, was a great castle, grey as the February noon, solid as the massive black rock from which it seemed to grow. Lower down from the black rock a petrified green waterfall dropped to a long, narrowish petrified green lake.

He had forgotten Edinburgh had a castle. He stared at it feeling as if he had been kicked in the chest and no longer saw it.

'If you come back in daylight look quickly left when you leave Newcastle station and . . .' '. . . Sure as hell, after the odd nine hundred years and . . .' '. . . Ain't it the truth, Chuck . . .' '. . . CHRISSAKES! . . . CHRISSAKES! . . .'

'You're just fine, hen, just fine . . . you've been in a wee accident . . . you're in an ambulance, hen – you're just fine . . .' '. . . Easy, mate, good and easy . . . oh my bloody word you take it easy, mate . . . she'll do right . . .' '. . . There, there, lad – none of that – you're doing all right . . . you're in a hospital, lad – there, there – you're doing all right . . .'

'Hi, there! Me Dave Oliver, you Francesca Turner . . . Fran suit? Great! How does it feel to be one of the ones that got away? . . .'

'Pulmonary embolus . . . yes, clot . . . yes, big one . . . yes, one of the main to the heart . . . yes, not often at her age but can happen . . . no, I've only seen two so young . . . yes, my father's seen more . . . no, I bloody don't . . .'

'You three must promise me you won't let this upset you – very sad – just one of those things – promise me you won't let it upset you . . .'

'Welcome to Surgical B . . . home from home with your three beds together . . . did you ever see such views of the moors? . . . I expect all Surgical A staff will be cluttering up this ward visiting you . . .'

They'd come cluttering. Ma Mastin, Doug, Preston, Yates, Sandra Gilroy, the student nurses whose names he never remembered as the students kept changing, Annie and Sharon, the nursing auxiliaries that shoved round Surgical A's food trolleys more often than most, Lady Mac and the Sir, Mrs Goodwin. Mary Hogg sent messages; she was awful glad to hear they were just fine; just now, the Oz was awful chuffed Jase's arm was coming along just fine; the Meredith was awful-fill-it-in-for-yourselves; the Cells were awful busy again; the boyfriend was awful impatient.

'Lost your way, young man? This is Medical B – oh! Well, perhaps, if she feels up to it. Take a pew on that stool whilst I find out . . . this way – manage all right? Just the one step down. Here's Mr Oliver come to call, Dame Ruth.'

Useful alibi, that step. She looked older than the Sir and her yellowish face was stretched tight over the bones. 'Always get a bit short of breath negotiating steps.'

'Bound to be a little tricky till you get the hang of it.' The voice hadn't altered. 'Come along, girls – as you were, nurses – heads up, shoulders back, soft hands at the ready for fevered brows. Nor had the eyes altered. Calm as hell. Seen it all and even if only understood the half it didn't do to let it get one down. Tomorrow was another day and next Monday was going to be a rather exciting, interesting day as she had never before flown in an helicopter or been a patient in any teaching hospital but St Martha's. Martha's, or the 'old firm' to Jase, Lady Mac and the Sir. 'Saint' to the DBE. 'I've never cared for abbreviations, Mr Oliver. So unprofessional and so likely to cause mistakes, but I expect you have to use them for speed . . . Oh yes, such a comfort to know Staff Nurse Hogg is escorting me to Edinburgh on Monday – such a good nurse – such a pity she never trained in St Martha's, but . . . oh no. Just a routine operation . . . good gracious, no! I've nursed far too many to successful recovery to feel anxious. Anyway, there's never any sense in flapping, is there? Flapping never does anyone any good but do tell me about yourself and your plans . . .'

'It was kind of you to come to see me. You've been on my mind . . . she did? How kind of Lady MacDonald. She told me your colour had much improved and it has . . . you do like spinach? Splendid. If you can't be bothered to cook it, buy yourself tins regularly – and do you like liver? Good. Yes, so nice with onions . . . I have enjoyed our little chat – oh yes, if you can spare the time, thank you. My love to Jason and regards to Mr Halstead whom I've not yet had the pleasure of meeting – careful on that step – well done, Mr Oliver!'

'Trying to get run in for lingering with intent, hen?'

'Hi, beautiful. Long time no see.'

'You know how it is. Cells full and –'

'Boyfriend panting?'

'That's right. All doing just fine I hear.'

'Oh, sure. I'm getting Seb Coe sweating, Jase is one-handling his wheelchair to the danger of life and limb; Mr H. is odds-on for balancing longest on his good foot and the physios are demanding danger money.'

'Great! And I hear you've been visiting the Dame.'

'Right mates, me and the DBE. How's she doing, Mary? And don't bloody dare say coming along.'

'Why not? Seeing that's the truth. For just now. What like she'll be this time next week is not for me to say as I don't bloody know the answer and nor does anyone else.'

'Fair comment. Sorry. So you're flying her up. Did you know she asked for you?'

'No! How do you? Not from her –'

'No. Lady Mac.'

'Oh. Well, then, when are they chucking you out?'

'Wednesday.'

'All the best – and to the other two.'

'Come up and tell them yourself.'

'No time, hen, and I've none now or I'll lose my new boyfriend.'

'What happened to the last?'

'Didn't fancy the waiting. No skin off my nose. Easy come, easy go, that's me. Mind you take good care of yourself, Dave.'

'You do that too, Mary. And if I can't waylay you again, thanks a lot for –'

'Getaway! Just doing my job. Goodbye for just now . . .'

* * *

'Not for "just now", Mr H. . .'

'Possibly, Dave. Jason watching television?'

'What else? Calcutta Cup's on.'

'So it is. I must go along for the second half.'

'Mr H. – why?'

'In my view because she is as kind as she is delectable, and remarkably wise for one so young.'

'It wasn't her fault! Hell, Jase said she did all anyone could've done fast as it could be!'

'Very true. But she did it – as seeing her again reminded you so strongly that you've waited two days to tell me privately of that meeting. Isn't this so?'

'Yep.'

'And neither you nor Jason require any reminder.'

'That's for sure, but nor do you for far stronger reasons. Yet you've just said you'd enjoy seeing Mary again.'

'So would you in my place and age. By late middle-age, Dave, either experience has taught you to temper grief and hope, or taught you nothing. The inability to learn from experience is a tragedy in itself and almost as great a tragedy as the lack of experience. You've to reach my age to appreciate that's the one that heads the ledger.' A long, long pause. 'It is for that last that I'm most saddened for that poór child. So young, so much to live for, but I fear she enjoyed little of her youth or short life – or am I in error? You were her contemporary. What's your view?'

He hedged, as he would have to his own father. The same standards, conventions, doors locked in early childhood now rusted, immovable. 'I go along with you. But – er – wouldn't say Jase has our outlook.'

'I'm not so sure. Quiet chap. Prefers to keep his thoughts to himself and deal with them in his own fashion. He needs time for the reflection that precedes the healing. So do you and – umm – not merely in this context. If you'll forgive the intrusion, have you had any communication from your ex-wife whilst in the Holydale?'

'No. Didn't expect it.'

'Quite so. Back to London, Wednesday?'

'Yes. The guy borrowing my Fulham flat says he'll move out. High time I got back to work. Self-employed. No sickness bloody benefit.'

'True. Does – umm – this affect your contributions to your ex-wife?'

'Don't make any. She wouldn't take 'em if I could afford it. Earns more than I ever have and probably will. Got her own hairdressing business. Small, but doing all right. Bright lady my ex and plays a clean hand. She's all right. I'll be all right when I get back to blowing the dust off my typewriter. The Almighty Oz is fixing for me to have my follow-up clinics in London. Save a bit of sweat and help with the beer money.'

'Hi, Lady Mac! Where's the Sir and what's a nice lady like you doing in a low dive like this?'

'Hanging around in the hope of standing you and me a cuppa. With, isn't it? And the most sugary buns this hospital canteen provides?'

'You've twisted my arm.'

'Good. Grab that table that's just about to empty over there . . . Enough sugar?'

'Just the job. We'll have to stop meeting like this, Lady Mac. And meanwhile back at the ranch –'

'The MacDonalds need your help. George has just flown up with Ruth Dean and Mary. I'm driving Mrs Goodwin back in the morning. Thank God neither Mr Halstead nor Jason need us around any longer.'

'And the Sir's just gone ahead as the chopper had a spare seat?'

'Ruth has no close relatives handy. We've been great friends since she, George and I were young together. That's why I want to ask you a big favour. Ruth has so enjoyed your visits and – no, not fussing as she wouldn't know how – but thinking about your welfare. She's concerned about your going back to your flat alone. She's convinced you won't feed yourself properly, and I expect rightly, if you live on carbohydrate gunge like that revolting bun with probably pub meat pies and a beer for afters. But I haven't pressganged you to talk suitable health diets for single young men. I want to ask if you can possibly postpone London for a couple of weeks or so, and come up to Edinburgh and stay with us. You mayn't believe the thought that you can drop in to visit Ruth and that I'm shovelling regular good meals into you can help her, or anyone, through a major op. – and I'm afraid that's what she's in for – but I promise you the most seemingly trivial things can help disproportionately during that stage. Also she knows this will give me something else to think about and that you make me laugh. Could you manage it? We've two spare bedrooms, a spare typewriter, stacks of blank paper, you've not yet seen Edinburgh and we all think it's time you did.'

'This major op. – er – cancer?'

'Yes.'

'God. Er – Jase knows?'

'Of course.'

'How long?'

'Cells.'

'He never said!'

'He wouldn't.'

'No. No, he wouldn't. Lady Mac – what – what –?'

'What are her chances? On paper, coming so soon after this business, probably forty-sixty. Knowing her as we do, more like fifty-fifty – and when she was nursing that was all any of her patients needed for her to pull them up and see them walking out on their two feet. She wants to live, Dave, and all her life, what Ruth Dean has wanted, she got.'

'That's not stopped you being worried as hell for her right now.'

'Of course not. Even Ruth can only have a finite number of heartbeats and I'm very fond of her and so are those I love. But I'm not only worried for her and them. For you, too, as I know I'm asking a tremendous favour. Right now, you're bound to feel you want to be shot of hospitals and all that reminds you of them. Can you face this?'

'Putty in your hands, Lady Mac.'

'Oh no, Dave. Not in mine or anyone's but your own. Aren't I right?'

'Never looked at it that way but – er – could be you read me good, lady. Right then. You've got yourself a deal – and thanks very much.'

'Thank you, duckie. Now, about Wednesday, I'll meet your train with great pleasure, or would you rather just turn up anytime? Chez these MacDonalds, any time means any time.'

'Like I've just said, Lady Mac, you read me good. I'll be on your doorstep Wednesday.'

'Stir yourself, Jimmy! This is it!' The taximan leapt round to open the door. 'I'll get the bag out the light then give you a hand. That leg's been playing up a wee bit on the drive has it not?'

'A bit.'

'Aye. Saw that from your face in my driving mirror. That's one-fifty-five on the clock – thank you! Ready? Great! That's you away out and here's the lady of the house coming to help you in.'

7

The April sun that a few seconds ago had been hidden by scurrying clouds and in a few seconds' time would be hidden again, caught the back of Mary Hogg's capped head and reminded Jason, standing a couple of yards behind her, of maple leaves before the Fall and of a holiday he had spent in Philadelphia with his mother's younger sister and her American husband in his second year as a houseman.

He stood in the shelter of the staff's side entrance to Out-Patients, and balanced his weight on his one armpit crutch to wave his left hand at the back of the hospital car carrying Mr Halstead and Staff Nurse Gilroy through the main gates and into the increasingly heavier traffic of the narrow hilly high street.

Mary waited until the car had disappeared to turn as if it were ten minutes and not ten weeks since their last meeting. 'Wouldn't you know it? Sandra's name got drawn out the hat to take him to London and she's from the south and I've not yet seen London.'

His smile was that of a polite stranger. 'You must get down sometime, Mary.'

She looked up at him and cursed herself for being half-deafened by her temporal pulses. She'd known from the start he was that tall and had those great flat shoulders and not the spare ounce. So he looked a right knockout with all the scars gone from his face and a good tan from all the time on Surgical B's roof balcony and the right stylish cut he'd had from the hospital hairdresser. Grow up, Mary – and watch yourself! She said, 'Our Mr H. has done us proud and you don't look too bad yourself.'

'No complaints, thanks.'

She glanced at the sling holding his semi-plastered right

arm and then at the walking plaster on his right leg. 'Top of the Oz's pops. And how've you been finding life on the other side?'

'Interesting and amusing, thanks,' he said politely.

Polite as hell, just now. Like his Dad – in the Cells – on that chopper ride. Not one extra word. Not one sign or symptom the old guy was human, till you took a good look back of his eyes. I'm fine standing, thank you, Staff. I'm quite comfortable in this seat, thank you, Staff. All just fine, thank you – and what if he was but having to stand there watching his one laddie broken and battered, or just sitting there holding the Dame's hand like she was his wee sister – and both times knowing all the answers and how best they should be answered and the back of his eyes showing the knowledge had him feeling like he was bleeding internally. In both, what could have happened but for a wee hope, hadn't. Jason's age had been in his favour; not the Dame's. A small smile lit Mary's eyes. From what they tell me the old lady's not bloody ready to rattle the pan yet, the grinning Oz had told Mary the morning after the old girl's op. in the Murrayfield. By then Mary had had the news in a short generous letter from Jase's mum. No secondaries, the whole primary out and God bless all at Holydale and the Murrayfield and Mary in particular. Mum was a nice wee body with no more side to her than Dad but easier to read – her eyes were a dead giveaway. So'd Jase's been in bed when she could see them properly. Not now, away over her head.

'That's great, Jase.'

He inclined his dark head in acknowledgement of the response to that question he had had from every member of the Holydale's staff with whom he'd had contact. 'How's with you, Mary?'

'Grand!'

'Good. Oh – someone said you'd been on a ward sister's course. Good value?'

She wrinkled her neat nose. 'If you fancy courses.'

He glanced at her face that was even prettier than he remembered. 'You don't?'

'Not when I've to spend them sitting around on my bum in lectures and groups hearing over and over stuff I've known for years. But to turn Grade 7 I've to attend the courses, so I'd to stick out the time. Not all bad. Every weekend free and a week's holiday when it finished.'

'Good holiday?'

'Just fine.'

'Good. And when do you turn Grade 7?'

She shrugged. 'Not sure I want to.'

'No. Not really your scene – as soon as you're a ward sister and worked the minimum necessary time you'll be plucked up into the higher grades, out of uniform and away from the patients.'

'No room in my dress pocket for my crystal ball, hen.'

'Stuff that. No crystal ball needed. You know damn well the brightest always get plucked up fast and that you're the brightest thing in the Holydale and, from the Holydale's hotline, in the Alanbridge health district.'

The compliment would have pleased her but for that 'thing'. So what else is new, Mary? 'Got me taped, have you? Nursing Officer Hogg. Ach, well. More in the pay-packet. I'll not gripe at that.'

He said pleasantly, 'If that's what you want, I hope you get it.'

'Thanks. Right now I'd best be getting back to my Cells. Due on twelve-fifteen. Ten past.'

He didn't want to detain her or need to ask for news of the patients presently in intensive therapy. From the time his walking plaster allowed him independent mobility, the Holydale's medical staff and ward sisters had adopted him as an 'almost' resident. He surprised himself by asking, 'Who are you on this afternoon?'

'Mainly the wee man in 2 – if he's still there.'

In 2 was a motor-cyclist with severe injuries to his chest and lungs; in 1 was a girl scooter-rider with a fractured skull, minimal brain damage and multiple fractures of both legs; in 3 a middle-aged hill farmer with a perforated gastric ulcer admitted during last night.

'He is. Both lungs have stopped haemorrhaging. The Oz was near cheerful about him this morning.'

'That's a break. When I went off last night he was hanging around 2 looking happy as a bastard on Father's Day.'

Her use of one of Benson's idioms made him smile. 'Sound chap, the Oz.'

She looked him over, gravely. 'So what else is new, hen?' She walked away without waiting for a reply, and he watched the naturally provocative swaying of her hips and the flicking of her slender ankles with an unexpected sexual appreciation. One of the few aspects of a patient's life that hadn't irked him had been the enforced celibacy. Old Halstead would have understood that, just as he had so much more. He was going to miss the old guy but for his sake was glad he had gone before he became too mobile. Not much joy for old Halstead had he been able to take a look at some of the other long-stay wards here, though they had illuminated for him why, fifteen months ago on his seventieth birthday, his father had announced he had no longer intended to fight his half-century's addiction to nicotine.

One evening in Surgical B when there had been nothing they wanted to see on television and old Halstead had been rather low, Jason had told him of that seventieth birthday. 'I had the weekend off and got up for the party. After the guests left, the old man produced an extra bottle of champagne he'd been saving for that moment. Had the toast on ice, too. He was all set to toast all the erudite, well-intentioned, senior physicians that in his forties and early fifties kept warning him that as he'd run on one kidney since childhood – hoicked out when he was nine or ten – unless he slowed down, cut out the fags, had regular checks and all that, he'd be lucky to hit fifty-five and anything after would be borrowed time. He never slowed down, or had checks, but he did cut from fifty-a-day for over twenty years to just under twenty and the odd cheroot. He said that night, "From now on, please, no counting and if I enjoy any more borrowed time as I have my past, I'll remain a most fortunate man. Right. Raise your glasses to all those worthy physicians that apparently overlooked the old medical maxim – rare is the happy man admitted with a coronary or carcinoma." '

Mr Halstead brightened. 'Sounds a remarkably pleasant occasion. Very pleasant couple, your parents. Remarkably devoted and well-matched, but those two seem to go together, in my experience.'

Jason having long guessed from Mr Halstead's unspoken

words that his wife's death had not been the unmitigated tragedy initially assumed by his fellow-survivors, had taken the subject on to Ruth Dean's steady progress. 'Incredible woman, Ruth. Scared the hell out of all Martha's including yours truly when she was running the shop, then had the lot in mourning when she handed over to the present DNS who's making a fair showing of the impossible job of following the Dame. Pity you couldn't meet her here though I expect you may in Edinburgh if she's still convalescing with my folks when you do your stint with Mrs Goodwin.'

'I shall look forward to the occasion – albeit, with some trepidation.'

'No need for the sweat, Mr H. Your missing foot, even if then replaced with the tin, will give you carte blanche. She'll see you as a patient and when she trained the patient could do no wrong, to his or her face. Never rubbed off Ruth Dean. Nor, I suspect, my mother, though she's never talked much about her nursing years.'

'And both ladies and your father met in Martha's?'

'Yes. Back in the war. This was years before my parents married.' Jason hesitated and then for the first time in his life found himself able to discuss his parents' first marriages with an outsider and without the process disturbing emotions he had previously refused to identify and would have been incapable of handling had he done so. 'When I was greener,' he went on, 'I thought Mum had the worst deal. Now, I hand that one to Dad. Mum had it tough as they come, but as she and her first loved each other like hell, I can now follow why she once told me if she had to live her life over again, she'd marry him as gladly as she did in the event. Different picture for Dad. Marriage fell apart from near take-off. Nothing in common but sex.'

'Regrettably, a not infrequent occurrence in war or peace. When did your parents marry?'

'January, '53. I showed up just before that Christmas and damn nearly repeated MacDonald family history. Dad's mother died giving him birth. He was an only. My mother was still on the danger list when Dad had to register my birth and gave me my first name.' He paused, staring at the outsize pink and white roses on the chintz bedcurtains drawn round one of the beds on the opposite side of the longish, wide, twelve-bedded male Bay. 'Mum's first was called Mark Jason. Martha's man. Dad's house-surgeon when he first met Mum. She was a night junior.' He sensed rather than saw the habitual discretion coming down like a curtain over the deeply furrowed, shrewd, watching face. 'Dad waited till I was old enough to catch on to explain why. He said that before they married, when Mum had been widowed about a year she told him she wished she'd had a kid as she would have loved the future to remember that once there had lived a young man called Mark Jason. Dad said, "He was my friend and a very fine chap. We had intentionally not settled on any name till we knew if we had a son or daughter, so when the choice had to be made, I made it. I had to wait to tell your mother and – she approved." ' Jason smiled shyly, and very sweetly. 'Not a man for the flowery talk, my old man, but I got the impression that Mum's reaction made him more than somewhat chuffed.'

'No doubt and deservedly. Not many men possess such generosity of spirit. Not that you require me to tell you that you have a remarkable man for a father. Nevertheless – umm – such good fortune can on occasions weigh heavily on the young. Many problems in that direction?'

Jason's smile altered to a grin. 'A few.' That was another first admission. 'When I got to Martha's after Cambridge, there were several consultants that had been his students, or housemen or registrars and a few that had been his contemporaries. The last lot obviously hated his guts and couldn't wait to get out their knives. "Mack's boy, eh? H'mm . . . oh, yes, I knew your father" –' he suddenly laughed 'and so did a few of the aged sisters. I only had to show up in their wards for the fluted cups to appear. Drooled over me. "Of course you've time for a cup of tea, dear boy! Just think! Our Mr MacDonald's son! How is the dear Professor? Such a pity Edinburgh coaxed him away. Oh yes, I knew your father!" Dad and Lloyd George.'

Mr Halstead smiled and idly watched a young nursing auxiliary sitting on the foot of a patient's bed across the way chatting with the patient and the ward sister standing beside her. The sight momentarily diverted his mind to that wartime ward in Egypt and what would have been the reactions of those young Army sisters to the suggestion that they, or the RAMC orderlies, should rest their weary feet by sitting on a patient's bed. Not dissimilar, he suspected, to Sam's dropping his musket at Waterloo. He returned to the matter in hand, 'I note with interest that you have the rare filial charity to forgive your father his success and equally rare wisdom for anyone your age, to appreciate that no man is too wise to marry unwisely.'

Jason looked at Mr Halstead in astonishment and thought of Gill Cameron who had made no further effort to contact him since their one telephone conversation in his first week in Surgical A. He had had news of her from Helen Cameron's frequent Get Well cards. 'Paul and Gill now really enjoying London and making many new friends . . .' 'Paul and Gill so enjoyed Easter in Greece, planning to try Corfu for their summer holiday – poor Gill so missed the sun in Edinburgh . . .' Strange, he thought, bloody strange but a fact that knowing Gill had finally explained for him Dad's first marriage, though it had taken a couple of nightmares to open his eyes to this, and to himself. On that last count he hadn't liked one bloody bit what he saw. He said soberly, 'Thanks, Mr H., but I can't claim either.'

'I wouldn't have expected you to do so, Jason. Only the unwise claim wisdom. Oh – are we in your way, Staff?'

'You should be in the dayroom with the other up-patients, my dears. You know sister doesn't like wheelchairs cluttering up the ward and it's supper in ten minutes. Come along – and you bring yourself, Doc. You may be a medic but you're only a patient in here and all the ups have to be at the table before a meal's served.'

Later that night in the more relaxed atmosphere that in Surgical B, as Surgical A, came in with the night nurses, Mr Halstead said, 'This life regularly reminds me of wartime soldiering. Common to both are long periods of boredom interspersed with short bursts of violent activity that occasion physical discomfort and sometimes physical danger, and long periods of enforced celibacy – where my age proves an overwhelming advantage, though I doubt this has disturbed you much owing to the many pressing matters you've had occupying your mind. Action being the enemy of thought and vice versa,' he added, avoiding looking at Jason for confirmation, just as he had avoided Francesca Turner's name in their many private conversations. All wounds, irrespective of their depth, were more tolerable without the application of salt. He went on, 'Again, in both situations there is the sensation of being in the grip of an all-powerful authority that has assumed total responsibility for one's housing, feeding, hygiene, and if hospital discipline is less obvious than the military, ultimate power remains in the hands of the C.O. – the Doctor. And daily orders remain nominally enforced by junior officers – the hospital doctors – with "Carry on, Sarn't-Major" replaced by "Carry on, sister, staff nurse, physiotherapist, occupational therapist et al." In both existences the most sensible course for the soldier-patient is to keep one's head down and if possible, suspend individual thought and judgement. But I suspect your profession has closed to you those avenues of escape. Though temporarily one of "them", I imagine you too frequently find yourself thinking as one of "us". Isn't that so?'

'Christ, yes.' Jason's self-derisive laugh exposed his very good, white teeth. 'Being a hybrid is turning me schizoid.'

'A disturbing experience but possibly of not inconsiderable value in your professional future.'

Jason nodded and thought aloud, 'When I'm clear what that is.'

Mr Halstead shot him a keen glance. 'Benson appears satisfied with the progress of your arm.' Jason said nothing. 'You're – umm – not?'

'Not that. Benson's opinion's more than good enough for me. It's just that – right now – I'm not too sure I want to go back to surgery.'

Mr Halstead received this without comment, or surprise. He had enjoyed this unlooked-for friendship with this intelligent, attractive youngster and had observed with approval Jason's ability – aside from the one tragic exception – to get on as well with women as men, and the depths of his quiet personality that, to Mr Halstead's discerning eyes, exhibited rather than concealed the underlying strength of the character. And throughout these long weeks in Surgical B, Mr Halstead had sensed that Jason had found himself approaching some major personal crossroads and consequently forced to reappraise all his previously held ideas, convictions and values.

Jason broke their companionable silence, to say, 'The problem of being one of "us" and specifically, as I've been, on the surgical side in a large inner-city teaching hospital, and even more specifically in a department like A. and E., is that you never have time to know the patients as more than injured bodies on a metal stretcher or accident table. Come and go. Some conscious, some not. Much the same in the theatre, only there, they mostly come and go anaesthetised. You get to know them in the wards, of course, but in the big places like Martha's the beds are in such demand that most long-stays get moved elsewhere. And whilst they're in, your main concern is the diseased organ, or busted bones, vessels, tissues. And there's some specialist for every bit. Not for the whole. Maybe, in the long-term, if you can cure the bits you cure the whole – but that now seems to me a hellish unsatisfactory way of spending one's life. Things were – or so I've been told – different in my old man's time. When he was Senior Surgical Officer in Martha's he was directly responsible for every surgical admission to the hospital. He was a general surgeon and that then meant general surgery. No SSOs in Martha's now. Senior Surgical Registrars running the various surgical units and each one polarized on the respective specialised bit. The nurses, in the main, still deal with the whole, but even that's being split up now so many of the more academically educated younger trained nurses are turning themselves into medical assistants or glorified technicians. This may be the right answer – but I'm no longer sure it's the answer for me. I'm beginning to think I want to deal with the whole – as people first and patients, second. I can't see my being able to do that in Martha's or any hospital. Have to get outside.'

'GP?'

'If I do, mean more training.'

'And that's not precisely the future you had envisaged for your father's son?'

Jason flushed but met the older man's eyes. 'Never, pre-Holydale. Could merely be my personal side-effect to being a long-stay. As I said, this place is turning me schizoid.'

'Understandably,' said Mr Halstead and, recognising

Jason's No Entry sign had gone up, changed the subject to Dave's latest postcard.

These cards arrived weekly for Jason, more occasionally for Mr Halstead. All had Edinburgh postmarks. 'Edwin the Saxon named this joint wrong. Not Edinburgh – Edingrad . . .' 'Your discarded thermals working a treat – but does it ever stop raining or blowing a Force 10? . . .' 'The Sir's fixed up my follow-ups at the Murrayfield and hoping to let Fulham and save my bank manager nervous breakdown . . .' 'The DBE now moved into your room, I'm still in spare, we take afternoon tea in the drawing room and slobber joyfully, decorously over your mum's cooking after hospital nosh – don't hurry home. Repeat. DO NOT HURRY HOME.' 'The guy borrowing my flat now paying regular rent – bank manager off danger list – hoping to move next week into flat belonging ex-patient of the Sir and going furnished for three months to suitable tenant . . .' 'Just tell me this, Jase. Why hasn't spring reached Edingrad? Must be an English plot . . .'

Ruth Dean sent them both Get Well cards. On Jason's, 'So nice to be with your parents again. Both looking well and all delighted you are doing so nicely. Am much looking forward to attending July's Congress in Canada and to seeing you long before I leave.'

The distance had prevented either man from having regular visitors, which distressed their fellow-patients, nurses and physiotherapists on their behalf, but not themselves. 'Real break not having to keep putting on the act, Mr H.'

'Quite so, Jason.'

What Jason, in particular, lacked in visitors was compensated by his avalanche of Get Well cards from Edinburgh and London. Every member of the staff in A. and E. had sent him more than one. 'Mrs Jim' had written a long, distressed letter, 'I'll never forgive myself for booking that seat . . .'

One of the physios had loaned him her typewriter to reply to Mrs Jim using two fingers of his left hand. 'Keep this quiet, Dr Mac. Can't lend it to everyone but you're almost one of us.'

Jason limped slowly out of Out-Patients and towards the

ground-floor gates of the in-patients' lift. The quiet of the patients' lunch-hour had settled over the little hospital, but he was in no hurry. He had chosen the cold lunch and the day sister on-duty in Surgical B this morning was keeping his tray in her office. 'Don't spread this around, Doc. Can't do it for them all but you're almost one of us.'

Almost. Almost able to walk unaided by that damned crutch. Almost able to write a kindergarten scrawl with his right hand. Almost a human being having for six years been one of us. He couldn't hold that against the staff as in those six years that was how he'd thought. Not consciously. Merely in self-defence. Had he not been able to give those innumerable mangled bodies the urgent attention they needed dispassionately, he couldn't have given it at all. And slowly, imperceptibly to him, what had started as a pose had come very close to becoming a personal attitude – until a few still unidentified young vandals transformed a few lives and ended more. For a time the Holydale staff had seethed with bitterness about them, but the only survivor to voice this had been Francesca. The rest? Jason shrugged and was too preoccupied to notice the movement no longer hurt. Must be rather like surviving some battle in war, he thought. What in hell was war but legalised vandalism?

The lift was waiting. He got in, closed the gates, pressed a button, absently. His mind was back in Surgical A. She had been an almost human until death blacked-out the 'almost'. After death, all human. 'So much worse when it happens to one of us, Dr MacDonald. Really brings home the "there but for the Grace of God". And don't try pretending to me you don't feel it, young man! I've eyes in my head. I can see you're right upset and you know me, always speak my mind. Just between us, I'm not ashamed to admit I'd a quiet tear in the sluice and as for young Doug – still sniffling. Don't say anything if he says he's got a cold coming. I'm not saying the lad's not got his faults but he's learning rightly and his heart's in the right place – which is more than I can say for some fathers but I'll name no names. None of that! You're having the tablets tonight and that's flat. You're getting a good night's sleep whatever you say.'

'You win, Mrs Mastin. And thanks.'

'Don't need thanks for doing my job, young man!'

Mary used to say that, he recalled as the lift stopped; he got out then found he had pushed the wrong button and was one floor short. But the lift had gone down. He didn't let that or the fact that he was not yet supposed to mount stairs without an escorting physio, interrupt his thoughts. He suddenly wished he had had more time to talk to Mary just now, without being clear why. He hadn't wanted to see her since Surgical A and had consciously avoided thinking about her, without realising, till now, the gap which seeing her again had just filled. He'd always known precisely why he had refused to think about her; she'd been too involved in scenes he had to forget or crack. Had she guessed that? Was that why she had kept away? If so, he could talk to her – if she wanted to talk to him. Talk; not spar; not swop endless futile cracks. Just talk, much as he had with old Halstead. Christ, he was going to miss the old guy during his remaining stint in Colditz-on-the-Moor. No one else here on his wavelength. Some of his fellow-patients were amusing guys, some of the women in the female Bay were worth a second look even if he had never had the urge to take it, but none that wouldn't have been bored and shocked if he really opened up. Easy to see what you are, Jase – one of the quiet ones.

'Dr Mac, what are you doing? I'm sure you're not allowed on the stairs alone! You medics! Give us all grey hairs when you turn patients!' The admonisher was one of the day sisters in Medical B, a small, plump youngish woman who cherished her reputation for radiating cheerfulness. 'We can't have this! Come and have a little sit-down in Med B till the lift comes back. You know how my old dears enjoy seeing you.'

Medical B, the one of the Holydale's two geriatric wards that still possessed, outside the ward, the roomy side-ward that had accommodated Dame Ruth Dean, had been partially restructured before the recent economic clamp-down. The former thirty-two-bedded long ward had been divided into two fourteen-bedded wards set on either side of a Nursing Bay that bore little resemblance to the one in Surgical A. The sister's desk was a solid wooden table with a highly polished top, around which were set four hard chairs and on either side, two small armchairs. The twin wards were spacious and airy, with the windows on one side overlooking the high street and on the other, the moors. The walls throughout were a clean cream, the window and bedcurtains pale pink in the women's ward; pale blue in the men's. At the far end of each ward little groups of armchairs were arranged around television sets; in both wards, the dayroom and Nursing Bay, the armchairs were fitted with clean, much-washed, attractive floral loose-covers. In those ward and dayroom chairs the patients sat quietly, mostly wrapped in clean cellular shawls, their white hair spotless as the fingernails of their arthritic hands, and their eyes bright with false hopes, or glazed with tranquillisers, or bleakly, helplessly, angry.

'We did try mixed wards. Not a success, I'm afraid, Dr Mac. The old dears get so set in their ways, but they really enjoy their little get-togethers in the dayroom when we can coax them along there. I'm afraid that little bunch' – she nodded to the women sitting round their ward's television – 'are our real diehards – but all such pets,' added the sister as if that was exactly what her patients were. 'But heavy! My goodness, how heavy! You can't think what it's like lugging them in and out of baths, beds, onto commodes, wheelchairs, tugging them into clothes, feeding them like babies. Some do so resent being helped – and us! But as I tell the nurses that is only because they are so angered by their own helplessness and have to take it out on someone. Comfortable on that hard chair?'

'Yes thanks, sister.' He glanced around with the concealed mixture of despair and fury always aroused in him by geriatric wards. The Oz called this one 'where they wait for the bloody hearse'. Thank Christ old Halstead never made it in here. Not that they weren't well cared for; or, from what he'd seen, both day sisters and their assorted staff of State Enrolled Nurses and nursing auxiliaries were not professionally kind and more than professionally patient. That this sister's Nanny-knows-best syndrome stuck in his throat didn't dim his admiration for her having held her present post for five years. But he had to look away from the faces of the old women sitting, waiting . . . and control the hideous thought – if something happened to Dad and me – Mum?

'I don't know how you've stood this, sister.'

'Oh, I don't know. They are such pets! Of course sometimes I tell my husband I can't face another day, but I have to come back. Someone has to look after them. Either their families can't cope, or they haven't any. And can you blame their families? Coping with a semi-bedridden, incontinent, mentally confused great-gran or grandad is a full-time job and demands real skill. How can young wives with kiddies and the part-time job most wives get soon as the kiddies start school, be expected to cope? Or the young grans? Most take full-time jobs soon as their families have left home, have very often coped with elderly parents for years and what with the menopause and one thing and another feel that at last they need a little life of their own before they join the queue for our beds. And, anyway, they need the money their jobs bring. Who doesn't these days? There's so much unemployment in Holydale – more for the men – the women usually seem to find some work, I expect as women'll take anything. Women are so much more adaptable, but' – she laughed cheerfully – 'not always in here. Some of my old grans are real tartars! As for my grandads! One of them spat his porridge all over me this morning – but he's not been with us long. He'll settle down in time – oh dear, off already?'

'That sounds like the lift coming up. Thanks for the seat, sister. I should get back. They're keeping my lunch.'

'My goodness, you are a favoured patient! But no trying those stairs if the lift hasn't waited. Can't have you taking risks!'

That's it, he thought, opening the lift gates. Omnipresent, omniscient Nanny – in a white coat, white uniform, blue uniform, unisex scruffy anoraks and denims, stiff collar and pinstripes, or the comfortable tweeds of the chap in the middle of the road you can trust. Trust Nanny. Don't take risks with your health; cut out smoking; cut down on the booze – it may cost infinitely more in money and human grief and crime than tobacco, but far too hot a political potato for any government to slap a health warning on a bottle of booze; keep up the jogging – hold it! Too many joggers springing coronaries. Jog in moderation; fornicate in moderation – but do remember to take precautions; why not get into the new discovery of the eighties – celibacy! Try celibacy – unless you enjoy it. If you do, stop it, at once! You clearly need psychiatric help! Cut down on the pressures; cut down on the stress; cut down on the risks; be negative! Forget life's a risk from the first breath and that few risks are greater than those incurred by unborn babies fighting their way down their mothers' dark vaginas. Trust all to Nanny who always knows best even though what Nanny says is best one year is not infrequently turned on its head by statistics, events, or both a few years later. Just keep trusting Nanny and then, if you're in luck and miss out on the wars, traffic, vandals, bombers, mechanical failures, clots and carcinomas – jackpot! A good golden tranquillised evening in Medical B and if you're dead lucky that evening can last for years.

The lift stopped at the top floor. He didn't get out. He pressed a button and went down to Medical B's landing. It took him twenty minutes to get up the stairs and once on Surgical B's landing he had to stop at the window until his respirations and sweat glands returned to normal.

That window was high enough to let him see the wide rolling spread of the moors surrounding the little town. The moors glinted with new green in the pale, erratic April sunshine and he looked them over gratefully, and breathing deeply. He had come to love the sight of the moors and the sense of space they provided in his present claustrophobic existence. Having lived most of his life in capital cities, only in this hospital had he slowly grown aware of his longing for space and began to appreciate his mother's seldom voiced nostalgia for the emptiness of the Fens.

Some place like this, he thought. Preferably in Scotland, but if not England, with hills or moors within walking distance and people whose faces and probably names you knew before they showed up in the surgery. Take a bit of time. The chances of getting some approved GP to take him on as trainee would probably be higher in cities – any kind of city – right! A few more years in cities, then out. How he would organise it all, he wasn't sure. But standing at that window he suddenly knew for sure what he wanted from his professional future and that somehow, he would get it. And he looked for a long time at his right arm with an expression that had never appeared on the face of the weary young registrar dropping into the backward-facing seat of a train about to leave Kings's Cross on the penultimate afternoon of last year. Had Dame Ruth Dean then been with him she would not have had to remind herself that the boy had been replaced by the man and that would have saddened the schoolgirl that for forty-odd years had lingered beneath her authoritative exterior. She liked to believe her friends remained unchanged, as it was beyond her imagination that the alternative to that form of change was stagnation.

His parents would understand. All they'd do, as ever, was stand back and leave it to him. When he had at school decided to aim for Cambridge and Martha's and not the University of Edinburgh, and the Murrayfield, or the Royal Infirmary or the Western General, he'd said, 'I think it's time I took an inside look at England,' and 'Fine,' they'd said. His academic record had got him into Martha's off his own bat, but he had never kidded himself his father's name had hurt his application. His opting out of Martha's wouldn't hurt the old man – hell, he, himself, had slammed that door far more spectacularly. All Martha's would do was fall about laughing. Always said he wasn't in old Mack's class . . . only one Mack of Martha's . . .

So what else is new, hen?

That thought made him smile quickly at himself, and then another expression illuminated his face and eyes. He gazed out at the moors in bemused wonder whilst his head tried to silence the heart that up to that moment he hadn't known he possessed.

8

Dr Meredith wore a defiant expression and a new cropped hairdo. 'I don't know what the Oz would say.'

I do, thought Jason. He'd tell you to stop mucking around like a moll at a christening and fix the bloke up. 'I think he'd approve.'

'That's just wishful thinking, Jason. He's been operating in Alanbridge all day, is off this evening and will kill me if I ring him just for this. And you are still a patient.'

'Only till noon tomorrow. Any help if I discharge myself this evening?'

'If you think that would help me –' She broke off, realising he was being facetious. She disliked facetiousness. Life was too serious and ugly for such an open admission of noncommitment.

'Lovely evening for a stroll,' he coaxed.

She leant her plump elbows on the stone top of the four foot high wall running round Surgical B's roof balcony that last year had been further heightened by three foot of metal meshing after a drunken nocturnal intruder had found his way up there and fallen over to his death. The meshing was very strong but fine and barely affected the view that was worth seeing on that early May evening. The sun was just leaving the clear, powder blue sky, the grey buildings of the little town had a pink glow; every patch of garden was splashed with yellow forsythia and daffodils, scarlet tulips, crimson flowering currants; a brilliant green cobweb lay over lawns, hedges and moors; and the two sloe trees on either side of the hospital gates had exploded into white flowers. 'It is rather nice,' she allowed.

'Too bad you can't get off to come along,' he lied to win and felt guilty when she blushed.

'Wish I could. Trust Dan Patel to get this weather for his half-day. You won't stay out too late?'

No Nanny. Nor accept sweeties or lifts from strange ladies – I should be so bloody lucky. 'What's too late?'

'Back when the night staff come on.'

'Hell, Merry, nearly eight now. At my speed I'll just make The Swan and back.'

'You won't get tanked?'

'Two halves at the outside.'

'They mayn't serve you. All the local pubs know the Oz and Co.'s anti to patients boozing.'

He glanced down at her face. 'Care to bet?'

She blushed again, this time with anger. Owned the world and knew it every time he shaved. 'All right. If you aren't too late.'

'I won't be. Thanks very much and if the Oz does get stroppy tell him I went into an acute can't-face-leaving-the-womb and that if you hadn't used the shock therapy first thing tomorrow I'd spring the cruel pain in me guts, the ugly palpitations and be ever so sorry, doctor, but far too poorly to face me breakfast or leaving me bed.'

She laughed. 'You sound like a Benedict's patient.'

'Why not? Just across the river from Martha's.' He wanted to tell her she should laugh more often, but didn't as he wanted to get out and not another long lecture on his blatant sexism. 'I'll push off now. Coming down?'

'Forgotten I happen to have a job to do?'

He smiled politely, 'Sorry. End-of-term syndrome.'

After a rush over Easter, the Holydale General had suddenly slackened. Invariably, he thought, going down in the lift. Either no chance to draw breath in any acute ward or department, or the whole staff standing around griping over the government's latest despicable, derisory insult of a pay offer. Whatever the offer, a despicable, derisory insult until the ambulances began queuing up and the pay-packets forgotten.

The electric wallclock in Out-Patients showed eight when he went through to the staff side entrance that was the shortest way out of the hospital. There were no patients around. The male charge nurse at the desk was doing the crossword in the evening paper. He glanced up. 'Wise old man. Six.'

'Nestor.'

'Doesn't – yes it does. Thanks. Taking the air?'

'Yes. No customers?'

'Don't ask for it. Take out – seven – got it! Extract.'

'See you, Charlie.'

The charge nurse didn't answer. He had to get 'assuage' in five.

Thursday evening. Pay-packets empty; pensions draining; schools and universities into the summer term; too much light and too little reward for muggings. Always Martha's quietest evening of the week. Only one parked ambulance in the yard and the two-man crew drinking tea in the porter's lodge, waved their mugs. 'Nice evening for a bit of sight-seeing, Doc!'

'Isn't it.'

He limped towards the open gates guarded by the exploding white sloes, the rubbered end of his one elbow-crutch soundless, the metal calliper of his new walking plaster clinking on the flags. Once out of the entrance he paused to look back at the uncompromisingly ugly grey building. As hospitals went – a nice little place – and one that when he had to remember it would be with deep gratitude and some affection. Only, Christ, the lack of privacy. Far worse than school as then he'd got back to his own room at home every night; even worse than Cambridge as there he'd had his own room on his stair and after his first term it had got through that when his door was closed he preferred opening it only to invited guests. He had not only the only child's habit of his own company, but a particular enjoyment and need for the solitude those from large families often equated with loneliness.

Like being let out of the nick, he thought, moving along the High Street pavement for once without an escorting physio. He liked all his physios, and, post-Surgical A, was more grateful to them than his nurses as from then it had been the physiotherapists that had done most for him. And the occupational therapists. His eyes smiled. If he had to put in more time on rush baskets, mats, bowls, he'd have the Chinese economy out of joint. 'You really are quite clever with your hands, Dr Mac . . .'

His tall, wide-shouldered, slim-waisted, long-legged figure in a loose dark blue rollneck and grey whipcords, right arm in a white sling, right leg in the now just-below-knee plaster showing between the ripped and safety-pinned lower seams of the right trouser leg, left hand gripping more than leaning on the elbow crutch, and the striking attractions of his black hair, dark blue eyes and strong-jawed face, drew sympathetic glances from the mostly elderly and aimlessly strolling early summer visitors. 'Poor young man – road accident I shouldn't wonder – and so nice-looking.' The local girls hurrying to evening dates in fair isle sweaters and denims speculated as to his potential once sling and plasters were off and hurried on, impatiently. The little groups of teenage boys at corners and in doorways considered kicking the crutch out of his hand and decided against it. No probation after doing a hospital patient; the big guy had one good arm and leg and looked like he'd use both; anyroad, he'd not have the bread. Never had from the hospital. Stood to reason. Nick anything from you in a hospital they would fast as you turned your head. They all said.

The television and radio shop roughly half-a-mile from and on the same side as the hospital stood on one corner of the entrance of Dale Street into the High Street. Dale Street was narrow and cobbled, with high narrow pavements, and ran steeply upwards. For a few moments Jason stood at the corner looking up Dale Street, then returned to the shop door. The 'Closed' notice was up and steel shutters down behind the glass door and shop windows. He rang the bell three times before a window a couple of yards over his head opened. 'Can't you read, lad – oh, it's you, Dr MacDonald!'

He smiled up at the firm, pleasant face framed with neatly dressed dyed black hair. 'Sorry to intrude on your nights off, Mrs Mastin. I thought this was your three off week until I heard in Surgical A this afternoon that it's your four. I'm off tomorrow. Just stopped by to say goodbye and thank you very much.'

'Well, I don't know! No one's ever bothered before! You shouldn't have troubled but it's really nice of you, Dr MacDonald! You can spare a minute to meet hubby? You wait there. I'll be down to give you a hand up.'

Whether he could spare the minute was an open question; that he had to, was not. Half-an-hour, two cups of strong tea, a large slice of homemade fruit cake, and half-a-pint of beer later he was back at the turning up Dale Street. He fitted his arm properly into the elbow-crutch and with his left hand still aching from the ex-Master-at-Arms' farewell clasp, took a firmer grip on the crutch and limped, slithered and clinked up the high pavement. This afternoon in Surgical A, Sandra Gilroy had given him the number of the Dale Street flat she shared with Mary Hogg and said she knew Mary would be in this evening. 'Like they say up here, daft as a brush is what I am. Left my keys in the flat, so I'd to ring Alanbridge when I went to first tea. Did you know she's been acting-sister over there last two weeks?'

'Yes. Standing in for someone's holiday, isn't it? But not living-in.'

'No. It was offered. She turned it down. Prefers getting back to the flat even though the round trip by the bus adds nearly three hours to her shift. On the 7.50–4.35 this week – up with the dawn every morning. She should be back after sevenish. No date tonight, she said.'

'I hope I can see her, if I can get away.'

Sandra Gilroy stifled the urge to retort, Not before bloody time and said, 'If you make it, don't waste time ringing the bell downstairs. Never works. But give the old bag watching from the ground front window a brave smile and loud groan to show you're not up to rape or she'll holler for the fuzz. Anytime we've a guy calling she doesn't recognise or fancy, she's out the front hall with her stick, and dinner-bell to get the neighbours across the road busy on their phone.'

He had assumed – incorrectly – that Sandra would have somehow managed to get another message to Mary warning her of his intentions to give her the chance of being out if she didn't want to see him. On past showing, he thought that last only too likely. Knowing even less about Sandra than he did about Mary, he underestimated the strength of their friendship, and the feminine capacity for remaining silent when the alternative risked hurting the feelings of a friend. Nor did he realise that well before both girls left school they had learnt never to believe anything any guy on the make said until his actions proved his words.

Sandra Gilroy was twenty-four, a Londoner, with the appearance of an unusually well-scrubbed, tidy schoolgirl, a dumpy figure, and the sharp wits and strong arms that had made her the automatic leader of her respective playground gangs in her primary and comprehensive schools. When Mary Hogg first moved to England after her second fostermother's death two years ago, the two girls had sized each other up at sight and a few weeks later decided to share a flat. Neither had regretted that decision. Their cramped but self-contained flat had two smallish rooms, one front, one back, and a tiny bathroom and kitchen. They had decided to share the back room as a bedroom and use the front as a living-room mainly to appease their elderly ground floor landlady's insistence that she'd have no hanky-panky on first floor. Both girls had, at other times, shared flats with young men and found they shared the conclusion that there was no percentage in doing all the cleaning up and cooking because you couldn't stand living in a tip and on takeaways, whilst paying your half and going short on sleep. 'When I wed,' said Mary, 'I'll wash his dirty socks with my tights. Not before.' Sandra said, 'If I marry, he'll do my tights with his Y-fronts and like it.' Mary thought he probably would. Wee Sandra was sexy as hell and a smashing cook.

Directly Mary got back that evening, she had a bath, redressed in a white V-necked sweater and old jeans with trouser legs wide enough to roll up above her knees. Despite the bath, her feet still ached. She made a couple of cheese sandwiches, and took them on a plate with a can of lager, her cigarettes and an orange plastic bucket two-thirds filled with hot water into the living-room. She had settled down on the small sofa with her feet in the bucket to watch television whilst eating her supper, before she remembered she hadn't plugged in or switched on the set. She couldn't summon the energy to deal with the set yet. She sat staring wearily at the whitewashed opposite wall, sipping, chewing, smoking in turn, then heard slow steps on the stairs and what sounded like the click of a stick. She didn't move. It was Thursday evening and would be old Mrs Wilkes from below coming up for the milk money. Mrs Wilkes always paid the milkman for them Fridays, liked a wee blether, and the money was waiting on the shelf just by the flat front door that opened into the living-room. Mary had unlocked that door after her bath. Sandra would be back soon and with it still daylight Mrs Wilkes would be on rapist-watch down front. She might be a wee bit slow on her feet but she'd all her marbles and eyes keen as Mary's first fostermother – 'Away wi' ye to the sink and scrub that muck off ye face or ye'll get the back of ma hand – and it's me that'll be having the wee word with the social worker and ye'll be away back where the like of you belong . . .'

Ach, what the hell? Mary sighed almost equably. Maybe the old bitch was right – she'd been but twelve.

The short ring on the upstairs bell was a welcome diversion. 'Come on in, hen! Door's open, money's on the shelf and my feet are –' Her voice stopped as abruptly as her face paled.

In the open doorway Jason leant on his crutch, grateful that his breathlessness after the stairs afforded the respite he needed to control his immediate reaction to the enchantingly absurd picture she presented. He had never seen her out of uniform. She looked younger, and so sweet and strangely vulnerable. He recovered first, 'You said come on in. May I, Mary?'

Very slowly she put down the can, a half-eaten sandwich and stubbed out her cigarette. She didn't move her feet from the bucket. She wasn't chancing standing the way her knees felt just now. And seeing what the walk and those stairs had done to him was no wee help. 'Feel free – take a seat – ach, not the blue, spring's gone. That's why the cushion. You get down in that and I'll bust my back getting you up. Take the orange chair – watch yourself, man! Have my bucket over your new plaster and the Oz'll have me for afters.'

'Sorry.' He lowered himself into the orange armchair and carefully positioned his right leg and the crutch on the floor. His chair faced the sofa and both were set at right angles to the one lowish window. 'All organised.'

'As well seeing there's not room to swing the cat – but who'd want to swing the poor wee thing if we had one? Would you?'

He shook his head smiling his polite smile and watching her colour returning to normal and wondering why it had changed. Surely Sandra had tipped her off? 'I hope you don't mind my coming round but when Sandra said you'd probably be in I –'

'Sandra said? When?'

He explained and was irrationally disappointed she wasn't here from choice as he knew he would have been far more had she had the choice and gone out. 'Just left the Mastins.'

She hid her disappointment. 'Grateful ex-p. on his farewell rounds?'

'Yes.'

'Makes a change. Put it in writing and I'll send it up the health board. Have them falling about with shock. You should see most the letters they get.'

'No need. I've seen some Martha's get.'

'Even the great St Martha's?' she mocked.

He hadn't come to, and didn't intend to, spar. He looked at her and said quietly, 'Stuff that more prole in every way than thou, Mary. I'm too old for it and you are far too bright for it.'

She shot him a strange glance, coloured and demanded, 'Want a beer?'

'No, thanks, but thanks for the olive branch. What's in that bucket?'

'Hot water.'

'Next time, bung in a handful of salt. Or better still, according to my old mum, vinegar. Worked wonders when she was a pro, she said. And after, rubbing the dry feet with meths. or surgical spirit.'

'I'll give the vinegar a try.' She smiled for the first time since his arrival. 'I mind your mum telling me she'd trained.'

'When?'

'Ach, sometime. We'd quite a few wee blethers when you were in the Cells. Once the Dame's junior. Rather her than me – getaway! There go a few more bricks off the roof. Forgot she's your godmother. Mind you, she was an awful good patient for all she'd the lot of us, including the Oz, in a right twist.'

He was interested and extraordinarily pleased that she did not seem to have the instinctive antipathy to his mother of just about every woman in his life since he had left home. 'My hotline's faulty. Missed that bit.'

'Trade secret, hen. Even my big mouth wouldn't have

let it out were you not good as gone. Driving down for you the morning? They'll be glad to have you back. And all doing just fine up Edinburgh, Dave says.' Her eyes danced. 'Has Scotland hooked that wee man! Any day now he'll be leading the SNP. Scots wha' hae in an English accent.'

'Won't be the first time I've heard it in that.' He was now extraordinarily perturbed, so sounded bored. 'Dave's been keeping you in the picture?'

'You know Dave. How could he not? He says the Dame's all but jogging round the block and your mum's having it tough keeping her out the kitchen.' She didn't add, and that you come not from a house but a dirty great mansion with enough books round your mum's drawing room and your dad's study for more than two public libraries and the whole joint reeking of not just upmarket security but real class. 'He's crazy over his new wee flat.'

'Good. Write often?'

'On and off. Not letters. Wee books. Pages. Awful amusing. Maybe I should keep them to flog when he's a big name. Started a novel – white hope of Eng. Lit., he says. You know?'

'No. Only had cards.'

'Doug's had a couple. One came today.'

'I'd forgotten he's in Alanbridge. You all get so shifted around this district that the only faces I knew in Surgical A this afternoon were Sandra's and Polly Preston's. How's Doug getting along?'

'Just fine. SRN now.'

'Good for him. Tell him congratulations, all the best and thanks a lot, from me.'

'Aye. Be seeing him tomorrow.'

'Thanks.' He studied his right leg. 'When are you next seeing Dave?'

She didn't answer at once. She watched his downcast, expressionless face and thought how often she had played this scene before, even if, before, it had been different. 'I've been nursing over five years, hen.' He looked up quickly and her green eyes mocked them both. 'I stopped fancying my male patients in my first year. In or out of hospital, I don't date those I don't fancy. You've too much between your ears to risk dating a patient, but when did you stop fancying yours?'

He met her eyes. 'I don't think I ever did.'

'Wise guy.'

'No. Merely a solid, selfish streak of self-preservation.'

The atmosphere suddenly altered in that small, shabbily comfortable and restfully but not obsessively tidy room. She said gravely, 'If not, you'd not be in that chair just now.'

'You think?'

'I know.'

He nodded to himself. 'Yes. You would.' Their eyes exchanged a silent conversation before he put some of it into words, 'I think – thought – hers was a bit dodgy. Worried the hell out of me, but it's only been with hindsight that I've identified the specific hell.'

Her eyes were greener, her face paler. 'Your fancying her won't have helped. Always clouds things.'

'Right.' They were still looking at each other. 'Didn't help her overmuch.'

She grimaced with distress for him and Francesca. 'Maybe not, though maybe not the way you're thinking if you're now thinking the same as Dave.'

He stiffened. 'Spell it out.'

'Dave's fixed she was a wee les. So's Doug.' She shook her head. 'That was the poor lassie's big problem. She'd have been much happier had she been right butch. She didn't want to like men Her dad was one. Fancying you made her real mad with herself and you.'

'She never fancied me! Loathed my guts!'

'Ach, hell, Jase! Don't be bloody daft! If you've not yet caught on to what it means when a bird keeps up the attack, it's time you did! Mind you –' her voice softened – 'you were just out the Cells and the danger list. Hard enough for anyone to think or see straight in a hospital bed, harder still when so bashed about and' – she tipped her head at his sling – 'with that to blow your mind.'

'Possibly.'

'Don't try that on me, hen. How long have you spent in IT? And I mean, spent, not just been in and out? I've had near two years in wee Cells here and Alanbridge. And I also happen to be a bird. Think I can't spot when the like to me fancies a guy, especially when both are patients? I'm not saying she didn't try to kid herself you were the original male chauvinist pig – or that you were the great love of her life. Just that she fancied you more than a wee bit and that's not love' – she looked at the window without seeing it – 'or so they say. It wasn't her fault she was all mixed-up and she'd taken the bashing and the shock too.' She faced him again as her whole mind was now on Francesca and Mary Hogg's attitude to those that were or had been her patients was in many ways identical to those of Dame Ruth Dean and Catherine MacDonald when Mrs Jason and Nurse Carter. Mary went on in a quieter, infinitely more mature voice, 'Maybe that crash was the way out she'd been wanting.'

His eyes darkened and his face grew rigid. 'You thought she wanted – out?'

'Niggled back of my mind.'

'And my subconscious.'

She sat straighter, 'That a fact?'

'Yes.' He told her of his train dream. 'I've not breathed this to anyone else. Sent me straight to a psychiatrist if I had. At the time, I refused to think it out, or accept it as a hunch. I've never gone along with medical hunches. Can't afford 'em in surgery – or, I can't. In my book, in surgery you've got to be dead clear of all available facts before you start cutting. But, Mary – that dream was so bloody clear. I couldn't forget it. I kept waiting for the bloody train to stop and her to leap off. Then she did.' He shuddered. 'So I'm a nutter.'

'Join the club, hen.'

'Huh?'

'Time,' she said, 'too many times, especially on nights, I've had this feeling I had with Fran – and every time, no matter what the prognosis, the charts, the monitors, the consultants – the lot – say – every time, no matter the patient looks to be doing just fine when I've this feeling – I know fine Death's waiting around. Times I'm not even sure which patient it'll be. I just know Death's around the ward, the Cell – and every time, *every time*, Jase – in but an hour or so, I'm doing Last Offices. But you keep this to yourself or I'll be getting the psychiatric therapy. Not that I'd be alone. Sandra, lots of other nurses have told me the same. Maybe this is the first time for you as this was the first time you've been stuck right there in the ward and not on the usual medics' in and out. When you're stuck right there days or nights like we nurses – makes the difference.'

'That's true.' He breathed as he had when he limped alone out of the hospital gates. 'I wish we had talked about this sooner. But you vanished. Why?'

Had he asked this when he first came in she would have hedged or lied. Not now that they had moved into the close professional relationship both had experienced with other colleagues on other occasions. 'Over five years' nursing. More than long enough to learn that the patients that had it toughest do best without the total recall.' She tapped herself. 'Part of it. Best to keep out the light.' She smiled faintly, sadly. 'It's aye the patients you've done the most for and that swear blind they'll never forget you that are the ones that forget you the quickest and have to. Old Mr H. caught on fine. Dave said in one of his letters.'

There was so much he wanted to say, so much he had to say, but he didn't know the words. He grasped at old Halstead. 'The old guy would. He didn't mention this to me, but he would. Wise as hell.'

'Aye. He was great! Tough about his poor wife.' She read the expression that flickered through Jason's eyes. 'Tougher for her than him.'

'I know. How do you?'

'Hen. I nurrrsed him.'

'Yes. I'm sorry.' He sat back looking at her with new appreciation and much more than a new interest. 'How in hell are you so wise, Mary?'

'Wise? Me? Wee Mary fra' –' She stopped herself and forced a smile. 'Getaway! You don't want my life and hard times.'

'I do. Please?' She was silent. 'Wee Mary fra' –?' he prompted gently.

She still hesitated, then thought, ach, what the hell? Get it off and finished. She looked at him straight and slightly raised her softly rounded, firm young chin. 'Right then. Wee Mary fra' the steps of Queen Street Station, Glasgow. Aye.' His face had tightened as if she had literally twisted his right arm. 'The wife of one of the cops that found me was called Mary. The Hogg came later. Adopted. They never traced my real Mum. Nor my real Dad, though I doubt I've the right to his name whatever it was.'

It took him a conscious effort to keep the compassion from his voice but he couldn't keep it from his eyes. 'How old when you were adopted?'

'Four months. Grand folks, my first Mum and Dad.'

'First?' It came out like a cry of pain.

'Aye. My adopted Mum had a coronary when I was ten.' She snapped her fingers, 'Like they say, come round in thirty seconds and you'll live. She didn't come round for the one though but thirty-seven. My Dad tried to carry on with a woman coming in and the neighbours. He was great. Had a good job. Fitter up the shipyards. Not a boozer. Just liked a night out with the lads. A few months after Mum he'd the few drams too many. Didn't see the car. Not the driver's fault.' She paused looking backwards and her vividly pretty face was a pale, sweet, sad cameo. She sighed. 'Back into care. Then out to my first fostering.'

He had to collect his thoughts before asking, 'How many?'

'Two. Problem bairn. Right wee tearaway – till my second.' Her eyes glowed. 'Jase, I was that lucky! Grand as my adopteds. Hooked on fostering. I was their eighth and they were awful good to me. It was like I couldn't believe it would last. It did. They had me telling them I wanted to nurse and got me working and not skiving at school – ended up with five Os and three Highers. Big success story. Social workers shouting for a raise. But when with my first fosters' – she held out her hands, palms upwarded – 'belted so often I stopped feeling it. Not the once after my first few months with my seconds. After I left to train I kept dropping round – we all did – like it was our real home. I'd just finished my general' – the light died from her eyes and voice – 'when that Mum was admitted my hospital. Ca [carcinoma] the pancreas.' She saw his wince. 'That's right. All over in the three weeks. And it was not five months after' – she suddenly looked older and for the first time he heard bitterness in her soft voice – 'he'd married again. I'd thought them so close – but just five months after. I never went back the house or met the new one. The job down here was being advertised so I just thought, ach well, let's take a look at the bloody English. Acute shock for this Scots lassie. The English are not so bad once you're used to them. I like it fine here.'

'I'm so glad about that,' he said sincerely, and sounded it. And then, for well over a minute he sat watching her in silence, mentally comparing her background with Francesca's, thinking of his burning sympathy for Francesca on this account and how, after her death the flames had been heightened by unreasoned guilt. Ever since January he had been haunted by his failure to help her – somehow – even though he could only have done so with words and been too blinkered by his confused emotions to see the simple unpalatable truth that none can help those that refuse help and enjoy the false refuge of self-pity. He doubted Mary knew the meaning of that last indulgence or the word 'defeat', which was one reason why she was such a good nurse. He knew he must now choose his words with great care and, with an unexpected and blinding clarity, why it was so vital to him that he should be careful.

He said at last, 'Figures now why you were working over Hogmanay and thank God for more than myself that you were. But you've added one figure wrong.'

She was watching him, tensely. 'And what's that?'

'You shouldn't be so hurt over your last foster-father's quick re-marriage.'

'How'd you know that, hen?' she snapped back.

'Admittedly, only second-hand, but from what I regard as a bloody reliable source. My own parents.' He told her the truth about their first marriages and seeing her expression alter, pressed his point. 'Took my father nine years to risk the repeat. Mum only eighteen months. It was my mother that once told me the highest compliment any surviving partner can pay the dead is to re-marry, soon as possible. She said only those lucky enough to know how glorious – her word – a happy marriage can be, know the absolute agony of being the one left, and that she thought probably this was even worse for men, as, in general, women are more used to being alone in the home. This bit was different for her as for Mark Jason's last three years they couldn't afford a home, she was working and living in a bedsit. But on the whole, I'd say she's got that picture right. Men go out to work then come back home and shout "Hi, I'm home" or something. And when they have to get back and open the door on silence, they just can't take it.

Got to fill the agonising gap and no slur. At least, not according to my mother and I believe her.'

She looked at him in silence for a long time. 'Mark Jason?' she breathed the name.

He nodded and gave the explanation of his name that he had left out.

'My God,' she muttered, 'no wonder she's as hooked on your Dad as he on her.'

'I know.'

'Aye. You do.' Again she fell silent, and then removed her feet from the cooling water and let her bare legs and feet drip on the faded brown carpet. 'Thanks, Jase – and for coming round.'

He knew it was time to go and pushed himself out of the orange armchair. 'I'd better get back or Merry'll have a cop car out looking for me.' He looked around vaguely. 'What's happened to Sandra?'

She stood up on her bare feet. 'Either having a blether with Mrs Wilkes below or gone along to the chippie.'

'Thank her for me.'

'Aye. Tell your folks all the best from me in the morning. How long up home?'

'A week. You've heard the Oz is handing me over to Martha's?'

'Sandra said. Seems they've new machines we've not yet got up here. Should speed up your arm, she said.'

'Yes. Only remaining problem. Leg's just a straight question of time.'

'Arm, too. You'll have your knife back that right hand by the end the year.'

'No.'

She shot him a clinical glance. 'Say that again!'

'No. Because I don't want to use it to pick up a knife. I want out. GP-ing. I'm going home to drop the bomb, though I doubt it'll upset the parents. But' – he grinned – 'Christ am I for it from the DBE. I've always heard she nearly did her nut when the old man chucked Martha's even although for a Chair. She'll blow all fuses at the prospect of yours truly doing a Doc. Findlay.'

She was too anxious to smile. 'Don't rush it, hen.'

'I haven't and I won't. Just do me a favour' – his voice altered to one she had never heard him use – 'stand around to pick up the pieces again.'

She smiled with her lips. 'Once you get back Martha's you'll need that from me like you'll need a hole in the head.'

'Don't bet on that, bonnie Mary.' He stooped and lightly kissed her soft, generous lips. She didn't kiss him back. 'Take care of yourself. Be seeing you, I hope.'

'Great.'

He looked into her eyes. 'That what they all say?' She nodded. 'Any good my asking you to spend your next days off in Edinburgh?' She shook her head. 'How about London? You've not been to London.'

She tipped her head at the telephone on a low bookcase top against one wall. 'Bill's paid.'

He was too relieved and too sad at leaving her, to smile. 'Good. And thanks, thanks very much.'

'Watch yourself on those stairs.'

Neither said more. She opened the door and watched his slow, cumbersome descent. At the front door below he turned back, propped himself against the open door and raised his left hand. She raised her right and kept it up until he closed the front door behind him. She let her arm fall limply to her side, quietly closed the flat front door and leant against it feeling as if she was once again ten years old.

9

Mary followed Lady MacDonald through one of the open French windows and onto the broad, riverside terrace backed by the great hospital. The height of the white, postwar wings, made the three old, grey, five-storey ward blocks look much smaller than they were in fact. Only the ground floors of the old blocks were presently in use; the upper were closed for reconstruction. The old ward windows were blank eyes; the old ward balconies facing the river, were empty.

One afternoon in Mary's first visit to London in July, Jason had got permission and the keys, and taken her up to one vast empty ward on the first floor of the middle old block. 'This was the old Wally's – Walter Walters Ward,' he said, 'where Mum was Ruth's night junior on that night in October 1944 that I told you about last night.' And they had stood in silence in the middle of that bare barrack of a ward and tried to imagine it with all the windows bricked in, all the dusty glass panels on the entrance and balcony doors covered with hardboard, and with eighteen beds down each side, two beds on each side of the balcony doors and ten emergency beds in a lengthways line down the centre. They had found that effort of imagination much easier than that required to picture Dame Ruth Dean and Lady MacDonald as twenty-two-year-old nurses, Professor Sir George MacDonald as a black-haired, white-coated Senior Surgical Officer of thirty-four. Even harder to visualise had been the ghostly figures of the SSO's young house-surgeon Mark Jason, and young Nurse Smith, the relief night senior, both dead long before the two silent figures in the empty ward were born.

The late afternoon September sun was hot as high summer, the ancient and modern terrace flagstones steamed visibly, and the stone-potted chrysanthemums blazed with bronze and yellow flowers. The river ran like silver oil alive with little boats, little tugs chugging by singly, busy as scratching hens, or hauling lines of flat-bottomed barges, whisking police boats, crowded pleasure boats. On the far bank the Houses of Parliament were sepia and not the dark grey of throughout her first visit, the redbricks of St Benedict's Hospital downriver on her left, had golden windows, and the whole massive London skyline had the powerful solidity and serenity of eternity.

Lady MacDonald, elegant in a fitted black silk coat over a black and white silk dress, with, solely to appease Dame Ruth, pinned to her right coat lapel the bronze star that was her old Martha's badge, rested her black suede-gloved hands on the warm stone top of the terrace balustrade overlooking the embankment. 'No gaps,' she murmured.

Mary, tall, slender, and transformed from prettiness to beauty by more than her soft cotton green and white flowered dress with a gathered waist, softly frilled collar and elbow cuffs, glanced at her curiously. 'Gaps?'

Lady MacDonald was surveying the opposite bank with faraway eyes. 'Bombsites. Most were still there when I finally left here for the second time in '49 and went down to Kent to work. Nearly, if not all, those modern buildings have gone up on the old gaps. Plenty of room.' She waved a hand towards the far right where Mary's height allowed her to glimpse the dome she could now identify as St Paul's. 'Specially that way. Two-thirds of the City was destroyed. From down here and even more from Wally's balcony back there' – she gestured behind her head without looking round – 'in daylight that opposite bank looked like a mouth with most teeth missing. Different at night.' Her voice was vague as that of someone talking in sleep. 'In the blackout on nights it looked like a mediaeval city filled with moats and jagged castles – incredibly beautiful when there was a moon. I loved emptying the damp linen. That was the junior's job and all the damp linen bins lived on the ward balconies. Getting out was the one chance of seeing the view and breathing clean air. Every morning on nights, me – and a few million others – used to look up thataway to see if St Paul's was still there. I used to hang over the balcony balustrade for a better look. It was there.

Like now.' Her faraway eyes looked upwards. 'All over the sky – barrage balloons with long cables looking like giant grey pregnant spiders trailing their long legs – but they were lovely in moonlight. They just hung there, great silver ghosts with long floating tinsel tentacles.' She suddenly blinked, then smiled apologetically. 'Sorry, Mary. Today's trip down memory lane has disorientated this venerable OM [old Martha's girl], but I'm delighted to have made it for Ruth's sake – glorious to see her so well – and to have been able to join in your pat on the back.' Her smile deepened at Mary's blush. 'Forgive my not warning you about that, but though I'd a hunch, I'd no inside news that it was coming. I couldn't have been more enchanted that it did. You deserved it. Still hollow inside?'

Mary stared at the river. 'Just about.'

Lady MacDonald looked very thoughtfully at Mary and then across to St Benedict's. She said lightly, 'One thing's sure. I am not the stuff of which Old Girls are made. This one's my swansong.'

Mary glanced up, smiling perfunctorily, then took a closer and clinical look at her companion's face. 'You're just saying that as it's so hot. You're awful pale. Would you not prefer to sit down?'

'No, thanks. I'm fine. Just the heat, though it's cooler out here. Hideously hot in the dining-room despite its size and the French windows, but fill a room big as Trafalgar Square with a few hundred chatting Marthas and in a few minutes it'd seem like the Black Hole of Calcutta. Incidentally, I hope it was all right my dragging you away from your VIP glory to look at the river?'

'Ach, yes! Thanks a lot.'

Lady MacDonald gave her another thoughtful look, seemed about to say something, but stayed silent and returned her attention to the far bank.

Mary returned to her confused thoughts and, from the open French windows behind them, the chirruping of hundreds of female voices floated out to meet the roar of the traffic sweeping over the water in waves. Women of all ages from her own to what could have been her great-grannie's – if she'd had one – and she must have had one, somewhere. And the lot got up like for the Royal Garden Party at Holyrood and with posh southern English voices and the posh English way of looking down their noses like there was an ugly pong. At first this afternoon – like in July – and having that drink in Sep's last night – she'd thought herself the pong and then thought, ach to hell, no skin off her nose. At first this afternoon, like all today till it happened, she'd wished the Dame had not asked her and that she'd not promised Lady MacDonald – and, oh, God, that he'd not been on that bloody wee train. She'd been doing all right, nothing special, but all right, till then. And even when – but a day or two from Hogmanay – she'd guessed what he could do to her she'd been able to handle it by keeping on telling herself he was a patient and then by keeping out the way. Until the turn-ups started and my God! Her sense of humour forced the laughter into her green eyes. If there was one she'd not have looked for in a thousand years it would have been to find herself stuck right in with this lot this afternoon!

'This lot' were the ex-St Martha's trainees gathered from health districts and hospitals all over Britain and not a few from overseas, and from homes with the small and capital H, to attend the annual September reunion of the Old Martha's Association today particularly celebrating the return to health of the guest-of-honour and most prestigious of all living OMs, Dame Ruth Dean. The occasion, as always, was held in St Martha's main nurses' dining-room, with most of the long tables removed, but a few left to line the walls on the left half of the great room for the serving of the tea that followed the official meeting. For this, the right half was lined with chairs facing a large, mobile platform.

'Not all OMs,' said Lady MacDonald when they sat together in the third row. 'Just approx. ninety-nine point nine percent. The others, as you, special guests.'

'Who'll the rest be?' she queried from politeness, not interest.

'DNOs, SNOs from other teaching hospitals, Scotland and Wales as well as England. Top brass from the Royal College of Nursing and so on.' Lady MacDonald's eyes lit, wickedly. 'Drop a bomb in here in twenty minutes' time and up'll go well over half the present Nursing Establishment.'

Mary was amused and reluctantly interested. 'That a fact?'

'Yes. Take a good look round, duckie.' Lady MacDonald

kept her voice very low. 'You may well not look upon such a sight again. There'll be a few men on the platform, but this is one of the last bastions of the all-female nursing profession and it's already falling. Martha's let in the first male student nurses two years ago. Jason tell you?' She read the answer and considerably more in Mary's eyes, but went on as if she hadn't, 'By next year the first men will have finished their general and turned into OMs – angels and ministers of grace preserve me – there's one of my set! Looks about eighty and she's younger than me. Oh, woe – where's my wheelchair and grey shawl? As I said on the phone – this is not my scene.'

Six weeks ago, on the evening of the day that, in the same post, Mary had received the official invitation from the District Nursing Officer of the St Martha's health district and a handwritten letter from Dame Ruth asking her to attend today's function as her special guest, Lady MacDonald rang Mary's flat. 'Do come if you can make it, and if the prospect strikes chill into your bones, you and me both, Mary. Not my scene. I've never been back to one OMA annual, but Ruth insists, quote, one really should rally round the flag, unquote. As they're honouring her, one has decided to grit one's teeth and rally. If you can make it and would care to come along with me, I'll be tremendously grateful for your moral support. We can fix the details later.'

Sandra Gilroy had been listening and watching Mary. After that call, she said, 'Right then, be a masochist.'

'The hell is, I like his folks. They've been awful kind.'

'And you've still three weeks' holiday owing.'

'I'm not wasting more of my holiday on that snooty dump of a hospital!'

'You will,' said Sandra uneasily. She'd been right before; odds-on, she'd be right again.

All the chairs had been filled and more brought in before the subdued chirruping was suddenly silenced. 'Any second now, enter the VIPs in procession,' murmured Lady MacDonald without moving her lips 'and we all stand as if in church but as we're not we clap them discreetly on to the platform.'

Mary made no response being then, as all day, too unhappy to care if they were supposed to let out a Hampden Roar. Then she saw Dame Ruth Dean, with the DNO of Martha's hovering at her side, leading in the procession. Mary's eyes glowed with the particular, overwhelming satisfaction of seeing a once dangerously ill patient back in good health that is one of the reasons why good nurses are nurses and good doctors, doctors.

Dame Ruth wore a French blue jersey suit, a bronze star on her right breast and her bare greying-brown hair neatly dressed; her only concessions to the scars on her left leg were flat heels and charcoal nylon tights. She walked slowly, as the occasion demanded, upright and graceful despite a slight limp and without a stick. The yellowish tinge had gone from her much rounder face. Mary judged she had gained about a stone since January. It suited her, so did this rave, but she wasn't giving that away. Just smiling pleasantly. And when she rose to speak and had to wait whilst this lot went mad and forgot the discreet bit and the clapping went on and on, she just stood there with her eyes as calm as when she had first surfaced to coherence with her head in a white cranial bandage, her face like a battered wife's and her life on a wee thread . . .

'I've been in an accident . . . dear me . . . hospital? . . . Presumably, intensive care . . . yes, thank you, staff nurse . . . I'm remembering – wasn't I on a train? Please – can you tell me if you've admitted a Mr MacDonald . . . very tall, dark-haired, young . . . yes, Mr Jason Ian MacDonald – thank God . . . oh, is he? How nice . . . thank you, quite comfortable . . . please, staff nurse, I'm not focusing quite well enough to read your label – what is your name?'

'Miss Mary Hogg, senior staff nurse in the Intensive Therapy Unit of the Holydale General Hospital,' said a voice in the present. The Dame's voice and she was still speaking. 'After all I have just told you, ladies and gentlemen, I know you will understand why it gives me great pleasure to welcome as my guest to St Martha's today the young trained nurse whom I regard as MY Staff Nurse Hogg.' She held up a silencing hand and smiled straight at

Mary's astounded face. 'Please, my dear, for the benefit of those at the back, would you be kind enough to stand up?'

Mary was too petrified to move until Lady MacDonald kicked her gently and whispered, 'On your feet, duckie!' She rose nervously, her face scarlet, eyes downcast whilst the lot clapped like she was Florence Nightingale's wee sister and she'd still be standing there had Lady MacDonald not given her skirt a tug. It seemed to take the rest of the meeting for her face to cool down and her to dare look around and wherever she looked they were smiling at her. When it was over, Lady MacDonald, grinning like Jase, whispered, 'Brace yourself, kid. More to come. This is where you join the VIPs for tea. I'll watch out and rescue you.' She propelled her to the one teatable with a space roped off in red, then vanished into the crowd. And there she'd been with the Dame and the other top brass passing her wee cucumber sandwiches and chocolate eclairs and meringues she could have swallowed in one bite had her throat not been too dry to swallow more than sips of tea. And all the time the tea-party went on, one side of her had been falling about with laughter at herself and the other had been right mad over the way she had gone around spot diagnosing without bothering to take the good look for what lay under the act.

Every patient conscious on admission that she had ever nursed, put on some sort of an act when they first came in. From her second year it had taken her less than an hour – now, minutes – to see through the act and know straight off what like of patient she'd to deal with. She could spot at sight the difficult, but they never stayed that with her, as she could handle them and they often turned into quite good patients for all that they remained basically difficult people. She was too professionally experienced to have any illusions about the reputed benefits of injury, illness and pain on the human character. She knew that in hospital beds, the brave turned braver; the cowards more cowardly; the petty, pettier, the stoic more stoic; and that it was the weak in spirit, not body, that went first to the wall and the fighters that fought, literally, to the last breath.

So long as she was in uniform she could place all and rightly, whatever the age, sex or social class and not just the patients. Staff and relatives. She'd got Sir George and

Lady MacDonald right from the Cells. If she'd not seen then for all the Sir and the Lady and the posh Edinburgh and posh English accents that there was no side to either, that they were awful grateful to her and she liked them fine, no matter what Jase had said and she'd wanted, she'd not have let him take her up to his home. Up Murrayfield she'd not felt lost without her uniform, but down here – not just lost but blinkered. She didn't know why, she just knew now, that it had happened.

She didn't know why, as whilst she knew her professional worth and had only to look in the nearest glass to know why she attracted men, she lacked personal conceit as much as she lacked any idea of her personal worth. She had accepted that her adopted and last fosterparents had loved her as all had loved children, but the older she grew the more she became aware that she had not properly belonged to either parents. She knew of, without appreciating the depth of, her own longing to belong, to have roots – to be like other people. She was too intelligent to be oblivious to the dangers in this longing to herself and her whole future. She had trained herself into trusting only in her trained self and avoiding becoming emotionally over-involved with men, and the combination had encased her deep, basic emotional insecurity in a new security until Jason was admitted to the Holydale. The tidal wave of her emotions had shattered the new casing before he was out of Surgical A. That the same had happened to Jason, if initially more slowly but now with the identical effect that was still increasing for both, she couldn't accept as she dared not trust either him or herself.

She studied Dame Ruth as they talked and saw that had she not nursed her, she would now be thinking the Dame was looking down her nose at her for not being a Martha and not having a posh English accent. No such thing! The Dame was a nice friendly old body and could no more help sounding like she was still addressing the meeting 'and mind you sit up straight and pay attention there at the back' than she could help being a good patient. And awful kind to have done and said what she had, just now.

Dame Ruth Dean was really pleased Mary Hogg had accepted the invitations; it had not occurred to Dame Ruth to prompt or underline until shortly after a telephone conversation with Catherine several weeks ago. Catherine had mentioned that she and Mack intended driving down to London for this weekend and dining with the Dean of St Benedict's tonight. Apparently the Dean, one of Mack's former, if considerably junior colleagues, and others in high places in St Benedict's, had been most interested to hear privately of Mack's high opinion of Mr Benson's surgery. It so happened that St Benedict's expected to have shortly a vacancy for a young consultant orthopaedic surgeon on their Staff and, of course, Mr Benson was a St Benedict's man. When Catherine rang off, Dame Ruth, as she put it to herself, put on her thinking cap.

A day or so later, at her own request, she had taken tea with the District Nursing Officer of St Martha's in what had formerly been the Matron's private office and was far more familiar to Dame Ruth than to its new incumbent. It was a smallish, elegant room lined with bookshelves, carpeted and curtained in silver grey. Carpet and curtains had been renewed during Dame Ruth's tenure, but she had maintained the old colour scheme with the old, still present, Matron's rosewood desk, since any alteration would have seemed to her gross disloyalty to St Martha's traditions.

'Credit where credit is due,' she said, having said why she would like to invite Staff Nurse Hogg to the coming reunion.

'Always your motto, Dame Ruth. And what a charming gesture to name her in your speech.' The two women looked at each other over fluted eggshell china cups. 'We shall all much look forward to welcoming her to St Martha's – as your guest. Glasgow trained? Yes – yes – very sound hospital – very sound training.' They exchanged another look. 'Naturally, none of us here – as in your time – would ever contemplate poaching a valued young staff nurse from another health district, but, of course, the young do find changes stimulating – another cup?'

Dame Ruth's imagination, though limited, had been enlarged on professional matters by long professional experience. Standing talking to Mary Hogg, she saw clearly that the District Nursing Officer's watchful, approving eyes were mentally fitting this nice, highly efficient girl in a St Martha's sister's uniform. How nice. A bit of a rough diamond, perhaps, but such a good nurse and every hospital – every St Martha's – constantly needed new young blood. Such a pity she had not had the benefit of a St Martha's training, but then – nor had Miss Nightingale.

'How about the adhesions, Dame Ruth?'

'No bother, my dear. Merely the odd twinge. Nothing to flap about. As for the leg – excellent union – forgotten all about it. Never does to dwell on these things,' she added cheerfully. She had long dismissed the train crash and her major operation from her thoughts. Dwelling on painful memories did no one any good. Last January she had been genuinely saddened for those that had lost their lives in the second carriage but she had not since then allowed herself to think upon them. Thinking couldn't help the dead, and, as it had been all her life, all her interest was in the living. She took the conversation on to Mr Halstead's increasing prowess with his new foot: 'Keeps in regular touch with Sir George and Lady MacDonald, I hear', and young Mr Oliver's splendidly uneventful recovery. 'Still up in Aberdeen? Or is it Shetland?'

'The last I heard from him was from Norway. He's away up north most the time. The new eyes and ears of the oil industry, he says.'

'Such an amusing young man and such a better colour last time I saw him in Edinburgh. And how do you find your other ex-patient in St Martha's today?' She noticed with approval the new tension in the pretty face. Any good nurse would be upset. Such a waste. Dear me.

'His leg's doing great. The arm's pretty good. Nerves and muscles picking up fast but he still has a wee problem with delicate finger movements.' Mary demonstrated with her right hand and the watching, listening, DNO nodded to herself. 'Grip's a bit weak, but improving. Mind, they've had to warn him here as Mr Benson did before he left us, that most like he'll have to try and avoid lifting heavy weights with that arm for life. He's over St Benedict's with Sir George, just now. Meeting Mr Benson down for the weekend too.'

'I didn't know. How pleasant for them all. Such a sound

surgeon, Mr Benson and so nice. Yes – yes, Jason will have to be careful about heavy weights on that arm. Dear me.' Dame Ruth's small sigh echoed another that was thirty years old. So like his father. Wouldn't alter his mind once he had made it up. Yet, possibly, as he wasn't his father, all for the best. 'Haven't you two just lunched with his parents? Great fun, I'm sure!'

Mary smiled with her lips. 'That's a fact.' Suddenly she wanted away. She didn't wish to seem ungrateful, but she wanted away.

She wasn't clear how, but as suddenly Lady MacDonald had joined them, was having a few words with the Dame and the DNO, and then in about three minutes the two of them were out on the terrace.

Mary leant her bare forearms on the warm stone balustrade and absently watched the panoramic view of the river. Another tug went by hauling a large flat-bottomed tarpaulin-shrouded barge. The tarpaulin was the size and colour of the one they'd used – after. Scene and sunshine vanished. She was back in the dark, icy, bone-seeping cold of that December night and standing shivering in her anorak with the hood up and her thickest pants, between Dan Patel and Kevin, one of the Holydale's Crash Ambulance crew, with the other official watchers and waiters in huddled little groups under the white glare of the emergency lights. Standing hours it seemed; standing, shivering, teeth chattering so badly you stopped noticing, then the urgent 'All stop! Someone's alive down here!' Then the deafening silence after the heavy-lifting gear had stopped, the oxyacetylene cutters and police radios had switched off; the chattering teeth had been clenched, and the frozen breath had hung like ectoplasm over all the suddenly upturned faces frozen to listen. And then – 'More than one! Up here doctors – nurses –'

She shivered violently and felt the sun again. She glanced sideways and breathed out in relief. Lady MacDonald hadn't noticed. But she needed a conscious effort to rebury the memory, and managed it because of her training. Then she glanced across to St Benedict's and once more scene and sun vanished. She could manage her professional, but not her personal memory and she was back in last night.

They spent most of the night talking. At five that morning, Jason got up to make tea. On his return he carried the tray on his left hand, poured the tea with his right, then took his cup over to the windowseat and flicked open the curtains. The London sky that to Mary never seemed to grow properly dark, expose stars, or be free for more than a few minutes of the noise of aircraft, was hidden behind a dark pinkish quilted canopy of reflected artificial light. 'Right,' said Jason, 'we've said it all. I want to marry you, you don't want to marry me, neither of us can tolerate the prospect of a long-distance part-time relationship, you want to stay north and pro tem I'm stuck south. You say – and I believe – that you love me but you won't believe I love you. You say you want a clean break and if that's what you want, right. No more P.M.s. If you ever, repeat, ever change your mind, give me a shout. If not, don't. I won't.'

'Don't look like that, hen –'

'Leave it, Mary.' His deep quiet voice vibrated with strain. 'We've both had all we can take. Still want to go back today?'

'Aye, but I can't till tonight. I've promised the Dame and your mum I'll go to this rave and we're meeting your folks for lunch. I can't back out on them.'

He looked at her lying in his bed under the navy-covered duvet that accentuated the exquisite whiteness of her lovely neck and shoulders. Her glorious hair was dishevelled, her green eyes red-rimmed and shadowed, her face sweet and indomitable as an early snowdrop that has just exploded through frozen ground. Ruth had been her patient; his parents, relatives of one of her patient's. And he'd been her patient, he reminded himself with a self-directed bitterness and nothing he could say or do could alter that. He said gently, 'No, you can't back out. Being you,' he added for the clarification he now knew was necessary. Having lived so long in England some of his many earlier mistakes with her had been caused by his having unwittingly adopted the English assumption that the common language had common implications to all that used it. 'With the Festival on I doubt there's a hope in hell of a last-minute sleeper on a Saturday night.'

'I don't want a sleeper. Waste of cash. I can sleep anywhere given the chance.'

He nodded wearily. There was no point in reminding her that his parents would gladly give her a lift back tomorrow and that as they were breaking the drive to stop overnight with friends roughly twenty miles east of Scotch Corner it wouldn't be much of a detour for them to take her straight to Holydale. They had dealt hours ago with that and their decision not to tell his parents she was cutting short her week's holiday. 'You get some sleep now. I'm going to have a hot bath and one of your cold cigs. Remind me I owe you a packet before you leave.'

'Watch those fags, Jase. Stop or you'll be hooked.'

'So what else is new, hen?' he queried drily and limped off to the bathroom.

She was too exhausted to stay awake and slept till mid-morning. 'Get any sleep yourself, hen?'

'Enough. Coffee's waiting. I'm afraid the toast's cold. Like fresh?'

'No, thanks. How long've I got?'

'About an hour.'

When she took her coffee and clothes into the bathroom, he went in to tidy the bedroom. The sight of the demarcation of her head on his pillows and the faint sweet scent on his duvet of her body that could be so loving and that he so loved, made him physically giddy. He sat on the side of the bed and put his head between his knees. No other woman had made him do that before; no woman before had meant a fraction of what he now knew Mary meant to him. She only had to be present to make his bones feel weak and the thought of life without her was more painful than anything he had suffered in the Holydale. Physical pain either killed you or, eventually, stopped. The mental pain of Francesca's death had been like a knife wound; short, sharp, then numbed. This pain came into a new category whose measure was beyond his experience or understanding, but not that of his instincts. Every instinct he possessed insisted that his head listen to his heart; that Mary was, and would remain for him, as unique as his emotions declared; that it was not merely a lover's fabrication and she really had come between him and his whole life before he met her; that the great liking he had had for her from the start had not just been the understandable reaction of an understandably very grateful patient, but had also been the instant recognition of a situation by an acutely shocked patient in the grip of the most powerful of all the primitive instincts, self-preservation, that had slammed on the brakes until the shock was long gone and sufficient strength had returned for full recognition to be both accepted and bearable; that now and always he must keep from her the fact that he knew he was presently being handed more than his own bill and would be happier than he had any right to be if she would only let him try to pay the lot; that he must leave the choice to her or lose her for good; and that he should have foreseen today would arrive from his first visit to Dale Street.

Ten days after that visit he had been sitting on the stairs up to Mary's flat when she got back from the hospital at a few minutes before five in the evening. He said without preamble, 'A friend of mine called Alistair has an old Rover. He's gone on to the Swan and is collecting me here at six. Martha's don't want me for another week, so I'm still home. Old Halstead's up visiting Mrs Goodwin but has to go back on Monday for the final fitting of his foot. He's doing nicely and so's the DBE. She's just taken off for friends down south and going on from there to beat up some nursing congress across the Atlantic. She's been getting her eye in on me which – er – could be why these last ten days have seemed endless but – er – I wouldn't bet on it. Our spare room's empty. My parents want to see you again. Old Halstead wants to see you again. Mrs Goodwin wants to see you again and – and I want it like bloody hell. Booked solid for these next two days off?'

Mary, fighting down joy and fear, demanded, 'How the hell did you know I'd be off and was back the Holydale?'

'Bell invented the telephone – or was it Edison? I also spent over four months in the Holydale.'

'Spying behind my back?'

'Fully licensed mole. How about coming back in the Rover? We'll run you back whenever you say – just one other deterrent. Dave's in Shetland and the great novel on ice. Someone's lashed out ready money for an in-depth on Sullum Voe. But he's doing fine.'

'Great.'

'If – er – if you can make it, my mother says for God's sake dress for the Arctic. Our central heating's on the blink. Yesterday we had snow and hail. Right now she's in her old skiing pants, one of my pre-teen skiing sweaters and we're all in our thermals. And she and the old man say please do come if you can. How about it, bonnie Mary?' His voice turned as urgent and uncertain as his eyes. 'Dated solid?'

'Ach, will you just let me think! Come on up – watch yourself, man!' She lunged to help him.

'Sorry. Thanks.' He had to steady himself on her shoulders and so had to kiss her. As she had to kiss him back, they both knew he had won that round.

She had seen such houses in Kelvinside on the west and Dumbreck on the south side of Glasgow, but had never stayed in one or even been inside the front door. None of the houses in which she had lived as a child, or since visited, had had proper dining rooms, proper drawing rooms. Just lounges, with sometimes a dining area, or sometimes a wee dining alcove off the kitchen. In her childhood homes, meals had been taken in the kitchen. And never anywhere had she seen a house with so many books. The books everywhere in that house in Murrayfield put her in mind of something one of the teachers at school, the one she'd most liked, used to say. 'You can always tell if any house is civilised by one look round. If it is, it has books and they needn't be in bookcases, or on wall shelves, they can just be piled on the floor. If they are there, whether the house is a palace or a wee but and ben, it's civilised. No books – and no matter how luxurious the house, how vast the colour TV and stereo equipment, how wealthy the owners, civilisation stops outside their front and back doors.'

Dave had it right. 'The joint's big as a mausoleum,' he had written in one of his letters, 'but mausoleum it ain't. It's a home and you can smell it's been one since MacDerby and Joan married and been got together with the kind of love and fastidious taste that goes so deep in both that they take it for granted. Jase must too. He won't know his own luck – how could he, never having known anything else? All the time I was there I kept feeling like that corny guy that knocked on the strange door then found he'd come home – only that home was a five-star hotel with the tender, loving, care thrown in for free. Had to keep pinching myself – but bloody peculiar spinoff from collecting a train ticket in a poker game, eh?'

Mary thought herself in no danger of needing a pinch. She'd stopped swallowing fairy stories before her teens. And then, on her second afternoon, whilst Jase and Alistair were out front fiddling inside the old Rover's bonnet and Sir George away to golf, Lady MacDonald told her to put her feet up in the drawing room. 'You're working tomorrow. Take the weight off them whilst you can. No, thanks, I can manage tea. Help? God, no, I don't need help in this house now George has retired and the phone's stopped ringing non-stop. I much prefer doing it with my machines and more than a bit of help from George. Nothing like surgery for making a man handy with his hands and for providing him with no excuse for not sewing on buttons. He sews back on all chez MacDonald. Go on in and have a breather. Kick off your shoes. I used to get out of mine directly I got back from work. Do you still? So that hasn't changed either.'

Mary went into the drawing room but didn't remove her shoes or use the sofa. She sat first in the winged armchair beside the lighted, powerful gas fire fitted into the hearth of the spacious fireplace. The fire had a pinkish marble surround and the white mantelpiece above was higher than Lady MacDonald's head. The drawing room would have taken the whole Dale Street flat without looking overcrowded if they moved out but a few hundred of the books lining the long, high, walls. It was an oblong, beautifully proportioned room with three tall, wide windows forming a bay that overlooked the small front garden, neat with pruned, frost-blackened rose bushes, a paved front path and a bare, low, frost-burnt front hedge. Beyond the hedge the pavement, quiet road, and quiet opposite houses were grey and solid and had the aura of an unassailable security that she had never known, and, as she realised at that moment with disturbing clarity, had always desired. The road ran across the long, lowish hill; behind the opposite roofs rose another orderly tier of dark-grey slate and glass cupolas and above, sprawling along the crest of the hill was the Victorian Gothic and twentieth-century concrete coglomeration that was the Murrayfield General.

She got out of the winged chair and drifted round the room she thought perfect for not being too perfect, touching the faintly faded blue brocade of the sofa that was soft as a duvet to sit on, touching the huge deep armchairs, the oval Queen Anne table in the window bay with the vase of hothouse red roses Sir George had bought yesterday morning. 'In your honour, Mary,' said Lady MacDonald as if that were true. 'Do visit us often, please. I love roses and yesterday's snow has put ours back weeks.'

She touched the roses and drifted on, running her fingertips over some of the books in the wall shelves, some of the bookcases, then with her handkerchief carefully removing her fingermarks from the glass. Despite that moment of disturbing clarity, just for a few minutes she let herself pretend that she was like other people and had a home and a dad to buy flowers because she had come back and this was her drawing room. Then she heard the front door open and Sir George's 'I'm home, Catherine!' and the immediate response, 'Lovely, darling! Tea's about ready. Good game?'

Mary, alone in the drawing room, went back to the winged chair by the fire that faced the windows, folded her hands in her lap, looked up at the Murrayfield General, thought of Francesca Turner and faced what she saw as reality.

She shouldn't have gone back. She knew that now. Instead – ach, face it, Mary – she couldn't keep away. She had gone back twice in June and during that third visit Jason had first asked her to marry him. 'Not today, but how about tomorrow? Next week? Next month?'

She tried to laugh it off. 'Just any time? And you with no job?'

'That side's all right,' he said, meaning, I've saved quite a bit of my pay as whilst working I never seemed to have time to spend it, when I'm home the parents flatly refuse to take anything, Dad gave me my London flat – in his words – in lieu of patrimony as dead rightly he's leaving everything he has to Mum as she's twelve years his junior and women usually live longer than men, and once Martha's have finished with my arm which they say should be late September or early October, even if it takes me a bit of time to find an approved GP willing to take me on as a trainee, I should be able to pick up enough from locums, weekend or night jobs to deal with the bills.

Mary, taking his words to be the dismissal of the importance of a regular pay packet by someone who had never had to bother about its contents, retorted hotly, 'If you think I'd ever live on or shack up with any guy happy to settle for hand-outs –'

'Who in hell's talking about hand-outs? Christ, we can't deal with this here – there's the car coming back. We've got to get on our own. Come to London, please! Come for the Royal Wedding – what better?'

'Can't. I've promised I'll relieve Preston all that week.'

'Come the week after. You must have some hols due.'

She had four weeks. 'Maybe I can get a week the end of July, but that doesn't mean –'

'More than that you want to see London. Fair enough – and – thanks very much.'

That first visit to London had demolished all her preconceived ideas of what would be her reaction to the English capital. Its overpowering size had invigorated, not overpowered her; she found the strangeness and quickness of the London voices fascinating, not irritating; the ceaseless roar of the traffic raised her adrenalin without giving her a headache; she was amused, not annoyed that the Thames was wider and grander than it had looked on television, and constantly enthralled by the constant juxtaposition of ancient buildings recognisable from newspaper, television and history book pictures, with giant new buildings. The crowded, bustling pavements recalled the warm liveliness of Glasgow. Never having indulged in nostalgia, she hadn't realised she had been homesick for city life until she found herself in this great, exciting, alien city. And she hadn't realised just what she had missed professionally until he took her into that bloody great dream of a hospital that had just stood there, a short walk even for him from his flat, since 1428.

And stood still.

The nurses still wore starched dresses and aprons and muslin caps with great bows up back, that previously she had only seen in old films about hospitals and that, like every female nurse with whom she had worked, she had yearned to wear in place of the new skimpy dresses, paper caps, and disposable paper aprons for dressings. The sisters and staff nurses still wore white starched collars and cuffs to their long-sleeved dresses, and aprons on-duty, proper starched aprons; and the lot rustled round with their noses in the air and voices hushed like someone had just told them Florence Nightingale was dead. She'd thought they'd enough medics in her Glasgow hospital. In Martha's, more white coats than you could shake a stick at, but she'd to look hard for one male nurse.

'Fairly recent innovation,' said Jason. 'The training school has a long enough waiting list to insist on five Os and two As for entry and most guys with that lot tend to go straight into medicine.' Sensing her reaction, he added quickly, 'Let's go over to Sep's.'

'Sep's', the nearest pub to the hospital, had another name, but he said that for the last hundred plus years had been known to Martha's by the nickname of one long-dead Dr Septimus Holtsmoor who was reputed never to have made a correct diagnosis when sober, or an incorrect one when drunk. 'Good old Sep', he said, as if the wee man were still alive.

Again and again in that week she had thought, he – and they (Martha's) – didn't know what time it was. They just thought they did having had fine educations and coming from fine homes and knowing which fork to use first and having a special knife for the butter. But they'd not tell butter from marge – never heard of marge. Like Dave wrote; didn't know their luck. She'd thought her Glasgow hospital had everything – like Surgical A. But after what she'd seen in Martha's, all the Holydale but Surgical A, most of Alanbridge General and more than a wee bit of her Glasgow hospital were way back with leeches. For the first time she felt herself in sympathy with Dr Meredith – like she kept saying, fit only for the knacker's yard. It wasn't right! What had Martha's ever done to have so much?

She had spent most of those weekdays seething with indignation and Jason, too in love for caution, added fuel by asking her to marry him, or at least to move to London, to share his flat permanently or till she got some place of her own, to give herself time to get used to the idea, to give him time to see more of her. Fortunately for both, he obeyed the instinct warning him not to suggest she apply for a job at Martha's. But that the nights had been so wonderful for both, heightened the tension for both. By the end of the week Mary had known she must get out and stay out or find herself tied to another dream that would blow up in her face like all the rest. Of course he kept saying it would not – what guy wouldn't say that when all worked up? She comforted herself with the thought that even if he meant it all, where would she be, twenty years' time? Ma Mastin. Ach, yes, she'd work full-time at first, then part-time after the bairns started arriving, and after, always get a job, but out of step, as permanent staff nurse. Was it for that that she'd trained?

She asked him not to ring her, but forgot to say, don't write. He didn't ring. Just wrote. She never answered one till last week's. 'Just heard you're coming down for the OMA. Couldn't you make it a week? I do miss you so much – please, bonnie Mary – please?'

She had come down two days ago for a week. The first twenty-four hours had been more glorious than either had anticipated. They had spent most of the twenty-four in bed. Last evening they had gone round to Sep's to meet some friend of Jason's from A. and E. called Bill. Bill had been late. Mary had not met him before nor cared for the encounter. Bill was a long, pale languid young man with, to Mary, a typically long, pale English face and snooty voice. 'Sorry I'm so late. Usual holdups.'

'Muggings?' queried Jason.

'What else, old chap? Friday night.' Bill looked at the bar clock. 'Just gone ten. On form. Thirty in when I got away plus two sliced throats. By the way, one throat was the old boy you stitched up on Boxing Night.' He ran a thumbnail across his throat. 'Your scar held up nicely.'

Jason looked rigid and Mary glared at Bill. 'Back in one piece?' she demanded.

'God, yes. He'll do and be back in with a third. Didn't

see who got him this time. Came up from behind again and got his wallet again. Poor old boy's hellish peeved. Over seventy but in pretty good nick – remember, Jason? Apparently the city fathers have offered to rehouse him but that means moving out and he's not having that, doctor! Bombed out three times in the war, he was, but always came back after and seeing as old Hitler couldn't shift him no young yobbo's doing that.' Bill smiled affectedly at Mary. 'Real toughs, these old Londoners. So you're from Glasgow?'

'Aye. We've a few wee toughs up there.'

'Dear girl, you need not tell me! Have I not seen the tartan hordes descending to collect the turf of Wembley? Such a quaint custom. Doesn't grass grow in Scotland? one asks oneself. But do tell me something I've pined to know – is the whole of Glasgow perpetually boozed or merely half the population?'

'You tell me first, hen – is the whole of London away out mugging, or but the half?'

'Touché, dear girl, touché.'

Jason said quietly, 'Will someone kindly remember that amongst those present is this Scots-Anglo schizoid.'

Later, in his flat, he said, 'Bill's a good guy only coming from New Zealand he sounds like an English pre-World War Two anachronism.'

'From New Zealand? Why didn't you say?'

'I like the guy. Why add to his hangups?'

'And what about mine?' she flung back and sparked off what ended at five this morning.

Lady MacDonald was still gazing across the river. Mary looked at her and then up at the empty balcony of the old Walter Walters Ward and thought of Jason's account of that wartime October night.

'They were all on duty when the news that Dad's first wife had been killed by a flying bomb came through to Wally's. He'd just left the ward, the switchboard couldn't find him, so Ruth took the message and had to break the news when he next showed up. No bleepers or walkie-talkies then. Phone was the one lifeline. Dad was up all that night – been up since six the previous morning after only about three hours' sleep and didn't get off till after nine on the second morning as an hour or so after his wife was killed a rocket landed close enough for the blast to kill Nurse Smith – she was standing by Dad when it got her – and send in about sixty rocket victims. Dad had to go straight down to Cas. I once asked him how in hell he kept going. He said in retrospect he didn't know, but in the event, just did and so did everyone else. Once he got off, they gave him a week's compassionate leave then sent him down to the country to take over as SSO in the largest evacuated branch of the hospital. He and Mum didn't meet again till she came back to staff in the general theatre in '48 when Mark Jason was first warded in our Thoracic Unit. She wanted to be near him and had to earn a living. He was in medicine pre-NHS. No social security then. Either you earned or starved. They'd then been married a couple of years but they'd been engaged since the early morning of that bloody October night. This last bit I only learnt from Mum a year or so ago. She said they fixed up their future in thirty seconds flat on Wally's balcony. Quite crazy, she said, as neither then knew if they'd be alive the next night, but that's what they did.'

'All empty now,' Mary murmured to herself.

'The old blocks?' Lady MacDonald turned slowly. 'Yes. The upper floors were in my time. We only used the ground and first floors.'

'Why was that?'

Momentarily, she stared as if addressed in a foreign language. 'Oh – well' – she gestured to the Houses of Parliament. 'Those were often the eye of the London target. Tremendous propaganda value, had they been flattened. Bombing planes, flying bombs and rockets hadn't the accuracy they have now. Would you have enjoyed being bedridden in upper floor wards under cracked ceilings and dodgy roofs knowing you were nudging the eye of the enemy's target for tonight? Plus, as most Martha's patients then as now were Londoners, knowing Martha's started the war with eight ward blocks facing the river?' She jerked a thumb. 'Ended up with that trio.'

Mary's quick colour rose in self-fury. 'I've kept forgetting the war.'

'Of course you have. Wars that are over before one's born are as deep in history as Waterloo. But having seen the old blocks knocked down' – she looked up at the new wings – 'and the mounds of rubble and huge craters from which those hideous monsters have arisen, does lend them a certain splendour. Very Martha's.' An ambivalent smile lit her pretty, worn, face and unconsciously she mimicked Dame Ruth's voice, 'Dear me, that was rather a rowdy one! Well, well, there goes Block 5 – not to worry, plenty of room in the basement – press on regardless and let's all have a nice cup of tea and get weaving on the rebuilding fund.' She heard herself and smiled apologetically. 'I shouldn't laugh, Mary. Ruth really was incredible, she genuinely never turned a hair, whilst most of the time I was bloody terrified. She helped the patients tremendously as they saw she wasn't afraid and that made them feel safer. She never had the slightest doubt that tomorrow would be another day.'

'You had.'

Lady MacDonald nodded soberly. 'Me, and more than a few others and I think for us the hangover lingers on and helps us to enjoy life more than most, as you do if you never take tomorrow for granted. And that, no one can, in peace or war. You just hope it will come and be as good, or better than today, depending what today's like, but you don't make the mistake of living for it as you know the only time you can be sure of is the present. And it's the past that shapes the present, not the future. All our pasts; all our presents.'

Mary glanced across to St Benedict's, then back at the old Wally's balcony and said on impulse, 'Jase told me.' She tipped her head at the old blocks. 'I hope you don't mind.'

For the first time since they had come out Lady MacDonald looked up at the old balcony and then she looked at Mary. 'No.'

In relief, Mary muttered rapidly, 'I thought that most like but couldn' a be sure.'

'I know. Like I'm not sure how you'll take what I must now tell you.'

Mary's tension returned, 'And what's that?'

'Whilst you were being a VIP, the SNO chatted me up to tap me on your professional plans. I hope you don't object to my telling her you've been offered a Grade 7 in

Alanbridge General but as far as I know haven't made up your mind about accepting. That all right?'

'Aye.'

'Good. Now, in her words, she would very much like a little chat with you before you return to Holydale. She's asked me to ask you if you could call in at her office at eleven-thirty on Monday morning and if that's not convenient to suggest some other time whilst you're down here. I said I've no idea of your plans but would pass this on and tell her your answer.'

Mary's intelligent green eyes were guarded as her tone. 'Did she says what's on her mind?'

'Yes.' She tapped her bronze star. 'I pulled the OPA and asked her straight out – sorry, duckie' – she saw Mary's puzzled frown – 'being back in England I'm thinking English – Old Pals Act. She didn't like it too much but she opened up as she knew damn well I'd get it out of Ruth before tonight's out if she didn't. She wants to offer you an IT sister's job, starting late October, and here that'll mean a two-year contract and the usual choice of living in or out. If living in' – she pointed to one slightly shorter, squarer white tower standing a little apart from the others that was tiered with long balconies facing the river – 'that's the new – to me – Home. All the sisters have balcony rooms and share the front part of the roof garden. Just over in those hotels on the far bank' – she waved across the river – 'people pay small fortunes for just one night in very similar rooms, but I think the view from this side tops all. What do I tell her? Or shall I just stall her with the perfectly understandable excuse that you've got a very tight schedule and can't right now say off-hand when you'll be free?'

10

They had taken their after-lunch coffee into the drawing room in which that morning Helen Cameron had redone the flowers for their return. The flowers were from their garden. There were gold chrysanthemums on the mantelshelf, multi-coloured asters on the early nineteenth-century china cabinet, and long-stemmed yellow roses on the Queen Anne table that, like the cabinet and its contents, had once been in Catherine's parental home in Norfolk. The roses were caught in the sunshine now coming in through the middle window. It was just two o'clock and the sun had at last dispersed the haar that had lain over Edinburgh like gauze on a mirror as they had driven in from the Dalkeith road a couple of hours ago. At this time of the year the sun would penetrate the left, most westward window before, from those windows, setting behind the green Corstorphine Hill; but shortly after next week's September equinox it would set markedly south of the green hill and from mid-November to late January its rays wouldn't directly enter that room at all.

George never noticed the darkness of the Edinburgh winters, the long white nights of its summers or what the weather was doing unless he was going fishing or the garden needed rain. 'Who was it said happy people never know if it's summer or winter, Catherine?'

She turned to him at once, her face absorbed in her own thoughts. 'Chekhov.'

He inclined his distinguished white head in acknowledgement, put down his coffee cup to light a cigarette and, from his seat in the winged chair, surveyed the pleasant, sunny, peaceful room with the contained contentment of a reserved man savouring the pleasure of having his wife and home to himself again. 'Interesting trip, but good to be back.'

'Lovely.' Catherine lay against one arm of the sofa with

her feet up and shoes off, in her customary posture when they had that room to themselves. 'Thank God, and that it's cooler up here.'

'Quite pleasant now the haar's lifted.' He looked through the windows at the profusion of roses in the front garden and the first deep purple dwarf michaelmas daisies coming into flower in the borders. 'I must get out there shortly. Turn your back for one weekend and up comes a bloody jungle.'

She smiled at him and herself. The weekend's combination of heat, socialising, emotional strain, and long drives had left her feeling the nearest human approach to mangled string. He had done most of the driving yesterday and this morning, but looked as if he had driven no further than round the block. And as so often of late, she noted with gratitude and wonder that his age had left unaffected his tremendous mental stamina. It had allowed him to appear tireless and to function efficiently during his fifteen years as an hospital resident when he had worked the kind of hours that would now have every resident in the country out on strike and had, in his time, literally exhausted to dropping point men younger than himself. That in youth and middle age he had never looked physically strong no one had ever noticed since then – as always – he had totally ignored his own health. In his early seventies he looked and was stronger than many men ten and fifteen years his junior. She said, 'Once again, George, I refuse to believe you were born in 1910.'

Pleased and embarrassed, he looked down his nose. 'I believe it whenever I walk into a hospital these days. Martha's now looks like an offshoot of the Yanks' space programme and Benedict's like a bit of County Hall. The whole ground floor seems to have been taken over by the bureaucrats. Even Benson was taken aback and he's only been away a few years.'

'He'd come out of the shock by Saturday night. Oozed content. Like me. I loved sitting there listening to the cheering ranks of Tuscany.'

'Glad you enjoyed it.'

'So did you, my darling – though your Covenantors' conscience refuses to admit it.'

His quick grin shed forty years from his face. 'As I've

frequently had occasion to remark, dear heart, it ill becomes one of a long line of militant East Anglian Puritans to disparage the Covenantors. Nevertheless – yes. Having spent my entire professional life fighting the bloody establishment it's not unamusing to discover myself apparently metamorphosed into one of its aged pillars.'

'Aged and apparently, my foot! A most distinguished pillar!' She gave a sudden little yelp of laughter. 'My God, between you and Ruth on Saturday I needed suntan lotion.'

'Your generosity never ceases to rejoice me,' he said smiling, whilst his clever, instinctively clinical eyes observed with concealed sadness how much the fatigue of the weekend and anxieties and additional domestic burdens of these last nine months had deepened the marks of time in her lovely, fragile face. 'On balance, Saturday worked out quite well.'

'After Ruth got into the act, God bless her. But lunch! Not even an axe would've dented the atmosphere.'

'A wee bit traumatic.'

'Wee? Blimey!' They exchanged smiles. 'Oh the agonising passions and traumas of youth! And, oh how unnecessary are most of these traumas. Thank God, George, if not all passion spent – all those sort of traumas long gone.'

He raised one elegant black brow. 'I don't recall our having any traumas of that nature between us.'

Her smile vanished and she nodded thoughtfully. 'We never had them. But by the time we married, between the war and our previous personal lives we'd both packed in enough traumas for half-a-dozen lifetimes. We didn't need any for kicks.'

'True, but by that token, I'd not have said Jason now harbours that need. The bellyful he's collected this year has matured him greatly. Understandably, Mary can't recognise this as she didn't know him before.'

'You're right, of course. Your diagnoses always were and are.' They looked at each other with simultaneously darkened eyes. 'The last belated traces of the boy were left in that carriage.'

'Inevitably.'

'Yes.' She sighed. 'This is one of the hells of parenthood. At any time you'd gladly give your life to save your young from hell, though you always know that until they've been through hell they'll never be properly mature or properly human. And those that miss out on the hell and reach old age, invariably end up still immature as children and usually beefing about their lifelong delicate health and bad luck. Never seems to strike 'em that no one grows old without being physically tough plus, and lucky plus. Both plus, plus, if your lives have covered two, or just one, world war.'

His face hardened. 'Indeed.'

Her face was dreamy but there was no happiness in that dream. 'Going back brought back all those men in Wally's – God, so many – and so many so marvellous – some my age then – some older but some younger. And all those women and girls in Rachel' – she shuddered at a memory that made him grimace as if kicked in the stomach – 'in both sides of that nightmarish ward in the basement – women – girls – with their faces sliced off by those bloody evil doodles.'

'By their blast. That did the worst damage as they exploded above ground.'

'I'd forgotten that bit. You wouldn't. Yes, I saw them still covered in blood and muck under the grey Cas. blankets after the students had carried their stretchers into the wards, but you had to sort out the mutilated heaps when they first reached Cas. and had to try and save – and often did save their sight though you're not an ophthalmic surgeon and their faces though you're not a plastic –'

'Many I couldn't, Catherine.'

She turned on him. 'Neither you nor any surgeon on God's earth. But, my God, you tried – with those damned doodles and rockets and with the H.E. and fire bombs and landmines dropping around in the three major and two mini blitzes. People now talk as if "the Blitz" was one isolated event! Huh! You had the lot!'

'No. I was in the country hospital for the '41 major.'

'So you were. I'd forgotten. Before my Martha's time,' she added vaguely and they fell silent thinking their own thoughts.

* * *

He had met his first wife during the first blitz when for fifty-seven consecutive nights London had been attacked by an average of two hundred enemy bombing planes. They'd married in the interval between the first and second major blitz that started in London, in May, 1941. Their married home had been in Warwickshire near the girls' school where his wife had taught English, but even had there been no war, the distance and demands of his job as SSO would have made it difficult for him to get home often. His alternate 'free weekends' had officially begun at 1 p.m. on Saturdays and ended in time for his Sunday night rounds. The train journey from the country hospital took hours longer, as he had to go through London, and that had generally involved long delays outside stations whilst some air raid was in progress or whilst debris left by the last was cleared from stations and tracks. Being a civilian hospital resident, his civilian's petrol ration was used up by one round trip home every six weeks.

In 1941 Catherine had been a full-time VAD for over a year in a military hospital in southern England and in the direct path of the Battle of Britain, and engaged to the local doctor's son from her home village, whom she had known all her life. Her parents had approved of the match but insisted that the young couple wait until Catherine was twenty-one to marry. Her fiancé, a RAF bomber pilot, had been twenty-one when his aircraft had been shot down over Bremen in that May. The combination of his death and the then obvious fact that the war would last years had resulted in Catherine's decision to train professionally and a few months later enter Martha's within days of her nineteenth birthday, then the minimum age for admission to the Nurses' Training School.

Sitting, smoking quietly in the winged chair, George's mind saw the thread of chance running through his own, through Catherine's, through Jason's lives, and pondered over the overwhelming part played by chance in all lives, in war and peace; and over how, to an extent limited only by chance, character determined destiny. His thoughts returned to his first wife; to the shock, grief, and above all guilt her death had caused him in the event and for years after. She had been dead nearly two decades before his intelligence had forced him to recognise that she had borne equal responsibility with himself for her death on that war-time night.

In the final weeks of their marriage he had been infatuated by Ruth Dean and, without telling her his plans, had written asking his wife to divorce him in the hope of marrying Ruth. To refuse his request in person, his wife had decided to ignore his repeated warnings to avoid London and south-east England during the flying bomb and rocket attacks. On the last afternoon of her life she had arrived unexpectedly in Martha's Casualty Department and asked to see him. He had been too busy to spare her more than a few minutes and she had then insisted on going down to her married brother, a Kentish farmer, for the night, with the intention of returning the following day to continue the conversation. Once at her brother's she had refused to share the family's Morrison air raid shelter and had chosen instead a mattress in the cupboard under the stairs. After the shot-down flying bomb hit the farmhouse all those in the Morrison had been dug out alive and relatively unharmed. She had been killed outright.

The news of her death, as finally, killed his infatuation for Ruth; and he had as effectively ended Ruth's for him first by telling her he wanted to marry her and then by insisting that he was responsible for his wife's death. Both had appalled her. 'Nonsense, Mack! I can't possibly marry – I'll have to give up nursing . . . Nonsense, Mack! You didn't start the war – you didn't ask her to come – she chose to come . . .'

Ruth, he thought, and a small affectionate smile lit his dark eyes. Long as he had known her, she had had an uncanny knack of hitting the right nail on the head without having any idea how she did it. How, or why. She had presently no idea what she was very probably doing for Jason and Mary and if – as he and Catherine hoped – those two eventually married, Ruth would be as astounded as when he had told her of his coming marriage to Catherine Jason. 'Good gracious, Mack! I know you've been sorry for her and helped her but I never knew you liked her! But – how nice and how wise. You should have a wife. Consultants and particularly Professors need wives – so much nicer for the patients and the staff – and she's just the kind of wife you need. I say – great fun!'

Four years before that conversation and in his third as a

general surgeon on Martha's consultant Staff – who had already been privately informed by the Professor of Thoracics of the admission to the Thoracic Unit and prognosis of his one-time house surgeon, Mark Jason – he had walked into the new Theatre Wing for his usual Tuesday morning's list and immediately recognised the new staff nurse waiting with him for the lift to the 'General' floor. 'Good morning, Mrs Jason,' was all he had said, and he had seen from the relief in her beautiful, expressive eyes that she had dreaded any suggestion of 'Welcome back' or 'Tough luck your husband's picked up tubercle' or 'Been a very long time since Wally's . . .' In general, he had always had the great sensitivity and great insensitivity that, so disconcertingly, often tends to accompany an exceptional talent for surgery, but from that morning in 1948 with Catherine, and later with Jason, the former predominated overwhelmingly. On that occasion she had responded with, 'Good morning, Mr MacDonald,' and when the lift arrived they had travelled up alone together in silence. But as he had followed her out he had realised why he had never wholly forgotten the disturbingly mature compassion in a look he had received from the junior he had thought of as 'that kid Carter' an hour or two after the news of his wife's death had reached Wally's.

She had come back into his life so quietly, he thought, watching her small, slender relaxed figure on the sofa, and come in like a sweet, lovely light that had illuminated his heart for nearly thirty-five years. And with each year the voltage had increased, he thought, and then remembered reading somewhere that the art of loving as the art of living improves with age, and nodded to himself. Och, yes.

She was looking at him. 'Mary may've turned it down. Too close to Jason.'

'Only for a very limited period. Even if he can get some approved London GP to take him on as trainee. London's a big place and he'll be pretty busy. But as I've been saying, I think what'll swing it for her will be the prospect of two more years at the bedside.'

She smiled very sweetly and sleepily, 'You'll be right, Professor.'

His eyes caressed her. From the first night of their

marriage her use of that title had been her especial term of endearment to him. 'I'm not infallible – as you bloody well know, my love – but I'll stick my neck out on this one. There's a wee touch of the young Ruth in that very bonnie lassie, but fortunately for Jason, only wee. One thing's certain; if he does eventually persuade her to marry him, whatever their mutual future may include, there won't be boredom. On either side.'

She laughed then stifled a yawn. 'Sorry.'

'My fault for keeping you talking.' He stood up. 'I'll deal with these cups then get out into the garden and you stay put and sleep till tea. I'll – och, no!' The hall telephone that was one of the extensions from the study, was ringing. 'Helen?'

'Bound to be.' She swung her legs to the floor. 'Can she come up with our keys and hear all about London. I must say yes – she's so kind.'

'Leave it to me. I'll take it in the study to explain the delay and say truthfully that you're resting in here and I'd rather not disturb you. Shall I suggest she and Donald come up with the keys for a drink this evening?'

'Do.' She lay back on the sofa and jerked up one thumb. 'God bless you, Professor.'

He smiled over his shoulder and quickly left the room closing the door behind him.

Catherine relaxed thankfully. A short sleep would sort her tiredness and she had never lost the invaluable habit acquired during her three years as a Night Sister of being able to fall asleep in seconds at any hour in any chair, sofa or bed, when she knew she could safely switch off and leave her world to others.

Her heavy eyelids fell shut and a smile that mingled great love and the private laughter that was rooted in long experience of life and men, illuminated her hidden eyes and uplifted the corners of her sweet-lipped mouth. All their married life; before; and long before; leave it to me, Catherine . . . leave it to me, Mum . . . leave it to me, Cath . . . leave it to me, Cathie . . .

Dave Oliver lowered his beer to listen to the chimes of Big Ben. 'Three. Should be rolling. Can't keep J.R. waiting.'

Jason smiled slowly, 'Watch your back, Dave.'

Dave tapped his nose with a nicotined forefinger. He now had an oilman's tan and short haircut, and wore the newish fawn denim safari suit he had won off a resting diver in Aberdeen who had assumed the wee Anglo too boozed to see his hand. The suit, he had just told Jason and Mary, had collected him a free lunch from the old mate in County Hall whom he had earlier arranged to meet for a pre-lunch beer. He drained the mug Jason had provided and reached for his stick on the floor. 'Look loaded and the world fights to feed you. Look in need of a crust – on your way, mate.' He stroked the stick. 'And this doesn't hurt the new image.'

Mary, sitting with Jason on the smallish brown leather sofa in his living room, surfaced from her private reverie. 'Why in hell are you still using that? You don't need it.'

'If there's one thing I love about you lovely liberated ladies it's your innocence,' observed Dave sliding his quick, amused gaze from Mary to Jason and recognising the mutual handshake in the watchful dark blue eyes without the slight surprise it would have caused him in the Holydale.

Mary demanded, 'Just say that again, hen!'

'Innocence,' obliged Dave. 'Not that that's how my old gran would've put it. Beat Ma Mastin by ten lengths in the not mincing words business did my old gran. Statistical rarity, she was – according to the statistics – though not from what she used to say. Working-class suffragette and never missed with her bricks. We got it for 'em she used to say, and they'll waste it, as too many'll prefer being doormats to being responsible for paying the rent-man and the ones that'll not be doormats and manage to grab the same educations and some of the same chances as the men will think themselves too high and mighty to think like women and be too plumb stupid to know they'll be thinking like second-class men. Men think like men, my old gran used to say,' he went on reflectively, 'and any man that knows how to think knows how to use what he's got. Women think like women and only remember to use what they've got, when on short commons. Give 'em a bit more and they start trying to forget they're women and wasting what they've got and been got for them. Bundle of hope, was my old gran – but could be she wasn't far wrong seeing the way women now seem to be losing hands down in the equal rights business.' He shrugged apologetically. 'Open door works both ways. You two know what letting in men is doing in hospitals. Male nurses taking over the top jobs from women all over. Same's happening in universities. Oxbridge women's colleges now have their quota of male heads but if you've heard of one female head of a men's college – tell me quick. I can flog it. Makes sense, if you stop to think. Men have been running the world too long – even if they have made a God Almighty cock-up of it – not to be old hands at taking over any shop once they get a foot in the door. Doesn't work the other way round.' He looked at Jason. 'Women have been in medicine roughly fifty years longer than men in nursing. Any signs of women taking over the BMA?'

Jason looked wooden and shook his head. 'My old man calls it the toughest trade union in the country, and he's right. In this respect, no different to any other trade union.'

Mary looked at her hands in her lap and stayed silent. She was too happy to want to argue and too intelligent to ignore the truth in Dave's comments on her own profession.

'Use what you've got,' repeated Dave tapping his stick on the floor. 'So I use this. Wrings withers, tugs heartstrings, has lovely kindly ladies falling about offering me seats on tubes and buses – and doubles as a bloody handy defensive weapon with a law-proof medical alibi. Clinch it by showing the fuzz me horrible scars' – he patted his right leg – 'gets even the Mets running me home in their cars. As of now – limping from here to eternity. But I mustn't get carried away or someone'll put a bomb in Grosvenor Square before I show up.' He rose from his armchair with the agility of a healthy man in his prime. 'Due at the Embassy at four. Time to roll.'

Mary wished she'd paid more attention. 'Why does this Texas paper want you over?' She saw the laughter in Jason's eyes. 'Sorry, hen. But I'm that –'

'Over the moon is the mint-fresh phrase you seek, beautiful. Join the club.' Dave stooped to kiss her entrancingly pretty face. 'All is forgiven if you swear to drop me a card when you're due up the Palace. I'll be down in the yard with my old mate Roger. Takes a lovely picture does my old mate Roger.'

She looked up at him. 'Don't wait on it. From what you've just been saying when I'm wanting the top my sex'll be against me.'

'Yours? I should live so long! You'll make a lovely DBE. My next year's tax on it. Like I've been saying and you've not bloody heard – once you're into a winning streak the cards play themselves and play right till the streak turns off.' He grinned up at Jason who had risen. 'Doesn't look from here like you're holding a duff hand.'

'No complaints,' said Jason with a calm that was contradicted by the passionate tenderness, hope and wonder that was in his quick glance at Mary.

Never, thought Mary, watching him tower over Dave, with the wonder dominating the hope in her own eyes. His Mum had it right. Life was today, not yesterday, not tomorrow and today was being so great – watch yourself, Mary – watch yourself! Ach away, no harm in the kick of seeing him looking so great in the clean white shirt with the tie he'd put on to come over to the hospital with her this morning and forgotten to take off as Dave had turned up unexpectedly whilst they were still talking. The shirt made his hair more black, eyes more blue and had his tan beating Dave's, but having long sleeves hid the brilliant and terrible scars on his arm. His black cords were off-the-peg, but fitted like they'd been cut by his Dad's fine tailor. He was looking as dead chuffed for Dave as he'd been for herself from Saturday evening. Whatever he was, he was no meanie to get uptight and sulk hours when others got the breaks like some other guys she'd known. Not just guys. Even Sandra – though by now she'd be mad at herself – last night on the 'phone, 'Bloody hell! Why should you have all the luck?'

She had never told Sandra, or anyone but Jason the full account of her childhood. It had only been in the small hours of Saturday night that she had nerved herself to ask, 'Your folks know?'

His encircling arms had tightened gently and the sudden tension in her soft warm body had made him want to shout with rage. He said gently, 'Yes. They also know I want to marry you and if you haven't yet spotted they're rooting for me from the sidelines you need an eye-test.'

She freed an arm and switched on the bedside light. 'They've been awful kind.'

He waited until he stopped blinking to raise his face and look steadily down into hers. 'They are kind, but this isn't only why they've been kind to you.'

'Ach, I ken well they're grateful I nurrrsed –'

'Very. Not just that, either. They think you – to quote Dad – a very bonnie, sweet, skilled and gallant lassie – and I've never known my old man hand a bouquet of that nature to any other woman but my mother.' Her quick colour had risen and he kissed her tenderly. 'Your childhood struck a personal chord for him.'

'You're not saying –'

He met her eyes. 'No. His parents were married when his mother died giving him birth. His father was an Empire-builder, worked in Africa, and owing to the climate and lack of modern immunisation therapies had to leave his only kid back home. Dad spent his entire childhood shunting between boarding schools, elderly relatives and the three years he spent in a kids' hospital near Glasgow – remember my telling you he's minus a kidney.' She blinked her great grave green eyes in answer and the vulnerability in their depths seemed physically to hurt his heart. 'I didn't tell you something I had from my mother in confidence. Dad's never talked to me about his childhood and Mum said he'd only once talked about it to her. He said then that whilst he was in that hospital it had foxed him why the rest of his ward was invariably in floods of tears after every rare parental visiting day. Parents weren't then encouraged to visit their sick kids, but having none to visit him that didn't worry him. What did was why the other kids let people see them crying as by then he had long learnt to hide and dry his own tears. He was admitted to that ward two weeks after his eighth birthday.'

'Ach, no!'

'Fact.' He paused. Then, 'He did buy those roses for you. Figures, doesn't it?'

Too moved for speech, she kissed him.

Sometime later she said breathlessly, 'If I get this job –'

'You will!'

'Watch yourself, hen!' She laid her hand over his lips. 'Not Monday morn yet –'

'Will be tomorrow,' he mumbled, kissing her palm.

'Maybe,' she risked allowing. 'But if I do get it I'll need to concentrate and –'

'Won't want one outsize MacDonald daily trying to twist your arm to marry him? I know. No problem. Soon as I heard the good news I knew that one had to go out of the window for two years if not longer. I won't like it, but I can tolerate the hell of a lot I don't like and will, rather than risk losing you. I know – I've always bloody known – what nursing means to you and what it would do to you if it was taken away – and what it would do to nursing. I'm not Ruth or my mother, but I was raised by one and saw a devil of a lot of the other and I have worked six years in one hospital and been a patient in another for over four months. Whether you know it or not, bonnie Mary – you are the future of the British nursing profession and one of its whitest hopes. Whilst the NHS can turn out nurses like you, there's not too much ails it – but there aren't too many of your ilk around, are there?'

She looked at him as if seeing him for the first time. 'You – care.'

'Of course I bloody care though, like you, only over my dead body would I admit it elsewhere. This is why I' – he slapped his chest – 'want out into the grass roots. Being a high-powered surgical technician is fine for those that enjoy surgical technology. I don't. Nor do I enjoy the bum-sucking necessary for clawing your way up the surgical ladder unless you happen to be as bloody brilliant as my old man when nothing and no one can keep you down. He went up like a rocket – as you are going for the same reason. But as you're a girl the one thing that could hold you down is marriage, once you have a baby or babies. Any time you want either or all three' – his quiet deep voice shook a little – 'what I said this morning will still stand. Pro tem, whilst you're taking over Martha's nursing establishment I'm getting stuck into the little black bag business. God knows where I'll find a job' – his strong jaw set – 'but I'll bloody find one once Martha's let me off the hook. And then' – his eyes laughed at himself – 'good old Doc MacDonald they'll say down the surgery. Means ever so well but mind you, can't expect him to know much if you're real ill. Got to see a proper doctor up the hospital if you're proper poorly.'

She hugged him. 'I thought I'd you taped and that you'd come out this GP freak when you came out the convalescence. No such thing! Rushing around with your wee bag sorting your patients' lives with their medical problems and knowing most often if not every time they aye go together, is for you! You'll do it just fine and they'll like it just fine and I'd you wrong. I'm awful sorry, hen.'

For a few moments he could only look at her and listen to the sound of a distant trumpet. Then he said quietly, 'Even Homer sometimes nods, bonnie Mary,' and switched off the bedside light.

She listened now to his asking Dave, 'What follows Dallas?'

'If I can swing it whilst over that side I want to get down to Venezuela. My oil mates up north say that's one joint where a guy can pick up his first million real fast if he's good and ready to work real hard. Could be well worth the look. Have to see what's dealt. No security in my business.'

'If there were, you wouldn't be in it,' retorted Jason. 'The only security you'll ever need, chum, is the security of insecurity.'

Dave shot him an oddly guarded and searching glance, then smiled. 'You read me pretty good.' He kept his relief over that qualification out of his voice and turned to Mary. 'You could do a lot worse than make an honest bloke of him.'

'I'll bear that in mind. But why've you not found yourself a new bird?'

'Feel free. Stamp on the ashes of my new, improved, gift-wrapped love-life.'

She was very concerned. 'Ach, not again?'

'I'll heal. My God' – Dave slapped his forehead dramatically. 'What have I got that has the homemakers homing in? There I was up top – and there was this lovely wee lassie fra' Aberdeen – and what did she want? The wee man working nine-to-five, home nights and washing the car Saturdays before being away to the footba' as the minister didn'a fancy car washing for the Sabbath. Never washed a car in me life. Encourages rust, I cry,' he added happily as that bit was true and he disliked lying to those he liked even although that had never stopped him doing so when the occasion demanded. Getting soft, mate, he decided seeing the concern in both their faces and feeling guilty. 'Too like my ex. Only one way out. Took off weeping for Norway and hoping she too'll find her insurance guy. Yep.' He answered their unspoken question. 'My ex has done it again. Just the job for her. Flogs insurance like it's going out of circulation, wouldn't be seen dead in an unwashed car Mondays and wears his face upside down.' He fingered his long narrow chin. 'Can't see this for hair and nowt up top.'

Jason looked fixedly into mid-air. 'Know him?'

Dave laughed, 'My best man. A man sure needs real good friends in this man's world. And that wraps up my life and hard times – mustn't keep the U.S. Embassy waiting.' He slapped Jason's left arm. 'Glad I stopped by for the beer and bonus. Give my best to your folks.'

'I will. Good to see you and all the best and – no – I won't add, take care as you don't know how. You just take note.'

'I'm this incomprehensible freak to those used to regular pay packets, mate. I fancy eating regularly. But take care, you two – oh yes – Jase, tell your lovely mum thanks again for rubbing up the lamp.'

Jason asked quickly, 'Mum? How's that?'

Mary had jumped up. 'Just wait till you've sorted that bit, Dave!'

'Sorry, folks, long story, no time. Stand by for the next soul-stirring instalment next time round.' Dave tucked his stick under one arm and made rapidly for the front door in the little hall beyond the living-room. They followed to watch him down the three flights from the open door. He was on the second when he heard Jason's telephone ringing and Mary's, 'I'll take it. The SNO said around three to four.'

Dave stopped to call softly up to Jason hanging over the iron balustrade, 'Bloody peculiar, eh?'

'Right,' Jason called back raising his right arm in the hail-and-farewell salute.

The flat was in one of a row of Edwardian terraced

houses that had been converted after the wartime bomb damage had been repaired, and stood in a side street opening into the main road running by the post-war main entrance to St Martha's. He walked briskly towards the main road, but at the turning stopped on the pavement, leant on his stick and stared unseeingly at the white shoebox towers blocking out the river and far bank.

No winning streak for poor old Mrs H., poor little bent Fran and those other poor sods. Nothing for them but – nothingness.

She didn't buy that.

'Don't ask me how I know you're wrong, duckie. I just do and I have all my life. Will you take umbrage if I pray for you?'

'Feel free, Lady Mac. Never waste any contacts going, I cry.'

He hadn't intended or wanted to tell her about the nightmares still nightly waking him in muck sweats in early March. The cast-iron excuses in the Holydale had been the heat and godawful noise made by the night staff and the other patients. No excuses in the silence of the Murrayfield nights. Not even a bird chorus up there. Just the odd solo.

One afternoon when they were lingering over tea in the drawing room and the Sir had just gone to visit the DBE up the hospital, she said, 'I'm sorry to upset you, Dave, but I've got to rub up my long-extinct lamp. Something's got to be done about this insomnia you're refusing to admit. How bad is it?'

He forced a grin. 'You know insomnia. Comes and goes. Like the 'flu.'

'It isn't. 'Flu is a disease caused by a virus.' She got off the sofa and seemed about to make for the light switches and then change her mind. She moved over to sit in the winged chair by his armchair, and in the gentle grey of the slowly expanding northern twilight and glow of the powerful gas fire, she looked astonishingly youthful, beautiful, and anxious. 'Insomnia's a symptom not a cause. The basic cause is obvious. What are the other symptoms? Nightmares?'

He had to look away. No one had been this anxious for him since his Gran packed it in. Not that anything else about her reminded him of his Gran . . .

He hadn't wanted to tell her, or come apart. He had done the lot.

She moved silently to him and sat on his chair arm, holding him against her whilst he wept on her shoulder. When he calmed down, she had silently released him, moved off then pushed a straight double Scotch into his hands. She returned to the sofa, sat with her back to the window and there wasn't enough light for him to see her face. Her silence was unstrained, soothing and lent a dream-like quality to his emotional exhaustion. 'Thanks – and sorry –' he muttered.

She brushed both aside with one small hand. 'You've got to write these out, duckie. Writers can sometimes, I'm told. I'm sure you can and you must.'

'Chrissakes – no!'

'Yes! If those few seconds of the crash is still too painful – you'll write that out one day – but leave it now. Write about what happened before – those Texans – the one that kept saying "Ain't it the truth, Chuck" – and how you feel about them.' She saw his violent shudder. 'My dear boy,' she said gently, 'I'm sorry, but you must or you'll crack. Please try.'

Thankful for the fading light, he gulped the rest of the whisky.

Solely for her, he had gone back to his borrowed room, fitted a sheet of paper into his borrowed typewriter, stared at the blank page and before he'd had time to convince himself his mind was blank it had flashed out a bit of schmaltz in banners. His hands, apparently working of their own volition, had typed it in capitals: REQUIEM FOR A TEXAS STRANGER. He had done the piece in fifteen hundred words, nearly needed a new ribbon and used up half a box of tissues. When he had shown it to her next morning, she'd wept, then insisted on taking it into the study. 'Made George grimace throughout,' she said. After that he hadn't needed her advice to send it out. He'd gone back up, made a fair copy, added his NUJ number to the title page and posted it to one of the Scottish nationals. It appeared in their features page a few days later and – bingo! Just about every national, commercial, and local TV and radio station in Scotland had given him a spot; the calls from London had started, and, after it was reprinted in the

States, the transatlantic calls. Dallas had got him in Stavanger last week. Come on over. All expenses paid, as for all the other trips since, and more cash than he had even thought himself worth when stoned out of his mind. Some of it – not much, just some – was the rate for the job and had shocked him into thinking 'Did I bloody write that?' when he saw it in print. If one of the many projects now shaping themselves came off, those bits might last longer than tomorrow's fish-and-chips wrapping. Two London publishers had already stood him lunches on the strength of his nearly finished first novel and whilst he still never believed anything sold until he saw the cheque, he'd stake all he'd earned from March on someone accepting it.

He blinked and saw the speeding traffic, the ambulances coming and going, the angular white towers. He heard the noise and smelt the smell of London with the sensations of someone trying to stop smoking and hearing the striking of a match to light a cigarette and smelling the smoke. New set of deprivation symptoms pushing up prematurely, he thought, and knew he was going to be away a long time. He'd miss London but as well to give it the break for a year or two. Under the protective colouring, Jase was far brighter than he, Dave, had gauged until after the March catharsis, and, as he had then seen, Jase hadn't only collected that from his old man; he had been bloody glad none of them played his game of poker – and bloody sorry he hadn't been born thirty years earlier.

Gawd! That was half-three! He looked urgently around then grinned and raised his stick at the solitary oncoming cruising taxi.

Mary rushed to the ringing telephone in Jason's bedroom. 'You could post us your measurements for your new uniform, Miss Hogg,' said Martha's SNO this morning, 'but much simpler to be measured whilst you're down here. Wednesday suit? Splendid. I'll ring you when I've fixed the time.'

She sat happily on the bed. 'Mary Hogg speaking.'

'George MacDonald here, Mary.' His voice was impersonal as an answering machine. 'Is Jason with you?'

'Just seeing Dave Oliver out, Sir George. I'll give him a shout.' She did so, then added eagerly, 'Could I just have a wee word with Lady MacDonald? I've great news that'll not surprise her but I'd like fine to tell her.'

He didn't answer at once and in the small silence she recalled the time and that it was strange such a good canny Scot had not waited until after six to ring London from Edinburgh. Unless there'd been an – and that 'unless' prompted a second recall with the speed of a computer; Jason saying '. . . Even those that hated my old man's guts have had to admit he always did his own dirty work.'

The machine again began talking, 'I'm afraid that's not possible, Mary, but as I can guess your news, my congratulations. Jason there?'

He was in the doorway looking a wee bit puzzled but happy. So happy! She must be way out – she must be! She had to be sure. She had to be sure. 'Is anything wrong, Sir George? Has there been a wee accident? Has Lady MacDonald been taken poorly or –?' but she couldn't finish as Jason had grabbed the receiver.

'Jason here, Dad. What's up?' he asked quietly.

She couldn't hear Sir George's reply. She didn't need to. She saw the colour and youth drain from Jason's good-looking young face, his eyes narrow to dark slits and his mouth set in a hard line as he took the full agony of the blow standing still as death. She had seen that look in other faces, that stillness in other figures and she knew what the cause must be. Knew, but – ach, no, no! The tears suddenly poured down her face and like a hurt child, she left them unchecked and sat huddled on the side of the bed tightly clasping her trembling hands. She longed to reach out to Jason, to take him in her arms, to try and help him – to try and help his father. She knew what this must be doing to Sir George – she could see what it was doing to Jason – but she could do nothing. Had Jason just been her ex-patient or some friend, she'd be standing at his side with one arm round him. But she knew him too well and had known grief too well to dare to move. She knew if he wanted her help he would show it and that if he didn't want her now he never really had, or would. And he would never really know what this was doing to her.

At last, Jason's voice, deep, steady and so gentle, 'Yes, Dad, yes, I – see. Did you say Dr McBride's now left? . . . Donald and Helen? . . . No, you wouldn't even want them around just now, but, listen, Dad – please – don't forget the shock of finding – er – is bound to hit you even harder in delayed-action – try and take it easy till I get up. I'll be on the first shuttle I can make – should be with you inside of three hours and I want – that is – I'd like to bring Mary . . .'

'Ach, please –' she whispered through her tears, but she wasn't sure he'd heard as he didn't look at her.

He went on, 'Yes, I thought you would . . . yes' – he screwed shut his eyes and his voice suddenly shook – 'Yes – she – she – would've hoped we'd have Mary – no, Dad!' His voice steadied. 'You're not to meet us. Leave that to me. I'll get a taxi at the airport. But, Dad, please – for Christ's sake, Dad, try and take it easy till we can get home. Thanks.' Jason lowered the receiver blindly and with his eyes still shut outstretched both arms to Mary. And in his gesture there was both appeal and protection.

George MacDonald, sitting alone at his study desk in the silent house in Murrayfield, put down his receiver blindly. Then he lowered the hand covering his lightless dark eyes and for the first time since, just over an hour ago, he had returned to the drawing room to say the Camerons would be round at six thirty and immediately he had opened the door recognised what had so quietly and serenely ended in his brief absence, he looked at Catherine's empty study chair.

Ended, he thought, and begun.

THE END

A WEEKEND IN THE GARDEN
by Lucilla Andrews

The second novel of the trilogy begun with
ONE NIGHT IN LONDON

June 1951 . . . it was a hot, hectic weekend for the staff of The Garden, the small cottage hospital in Kent, where antibiotics were regarded as the new wonderdrugs and the patients' wireless headphones a luxury . . .

Catherine Jason had become a theatre sister at The Garden to be near her sick husband, Mark, a patient at the TB clinic nearby. Also working at The Garden, as a locum, was Dr George Macdonald, an old colleague of the Jason's who has fallen deeply in love with Catherine . . .

As the weekend passed Catherine and George realised that for them, nothing would ever be the same again . . .

'Compulsive reading . . . is a vivid reminder of life in the immediate post-war years and of the conditions in which nurses worked'
Nursing Times

0 552 11909 1 95p

THE PRINT PETTICOAT
by Lucilla Andrews

In the country Maternity Unit of a London teaching hospital, Joanna Anthony enjoyed both her job as nursery staff nurse, and her love for the man who had been her 'steady' for five years. Two other young men, one an old friend, the other a new one, watched and shared her hectically busy professional life.

When she moved back to London to share a flat with her great friend Beth (and wallow in the luxury of 'living out of hospital' for the first time) Allan and Marcus were regular 'droppers in'. And then a serious illness took her back to her parent hospital as a patient, and in a hospital bed she finally faced reality — and happiness . . .

0 552 11385 9 75p